ETHIC IV

BY

ASHLEY ANTOINETTE

Ashley Antoinette Inc.
P.O. Box 181048
Utica, MI 48318

ISBN: 978-1-7328313-4-6

Trade Paperback Printing December 2018
Printed in the United States of America

Distributed by Ashley Antoinette Inc.
Submit Wholesale Orders to:
owl.aac@gmail.com

ETHIC IV PLAY LIST

Superman, Monica
A Couple of Forevers, Chrisette Michele
Little Lady, Mali Music
When We, Tank
Chanté's Got a Man, Chanté Moore
Officially Missing You, Tamia
I Love Me Some Him, Toni Braxton
Just Be a Man About It, Toni Braxton
Mad, Ne-Yo
Cry, K. Michelle
All Mine, Kanye West
Back That Azz Up, Juvenile
Get It Together, 702
Teachme, Musiq Soulchild
Deserve U More, Musiq Soulchild
Breaks My Heart, Monica
Own It, Ella Mai
One in a Million, Aaliyah
Everything, Ella Mai

LETTER TO THE FANS

Can you believe we've all been stuck on this ride for four books? It's terrifying yet exhilarating all at the same time. Ethic and Alani are beautiful. I have no other words for their journey thus far except that. I just love them. Thank you for investing in my art...for crying real tears...for laughing joyously...for falling in love more and more with every flip of the page. In ten years, we'll be looking back on this era and hopefully you'll say, "Wow. Remember when Ashley Antoinette released four books back to back that made us lose touch with reality?" Hopefully this art is impactful and lasting. I pray it leaves your heart open, your insecurities erased, and your soul exposed. Lastly, I hope Ethic makes you believe in love after pain. You know the routine. Grab your wine. Load your playlist. Flip the page and put the real world on pause. Ethic wants all of your attention. He's missed you. He needs you. Thank you for letting me turn ink into love.

s/o to Bianca on that one ;)

-xoxo-
Ashley Antoinette

s/o to Ashley Jackson for keeping your eyes keen and your heart open while test reading this series. I appreciate the glimpse you give me into your mind. Witnessing your reaction to my words before anyone else gets to read them is so insightful. Thank you. You're the best.

WARNING

This series has been known to cause *The Ethic Effect*. If you experience shortness of breath, palpitations of the heart, day dreaming, overactive emotions, out of body episodes, lustful thinking, or inexplicable yearning for an imaginary man/woman...find your book bestie and discuss immediately.

Happy Reading!

CHAPTER 1

I t's going to be fine, Ethic. I promise," Alani whispered, as she sat beside him. Ethic looked at her, reveling in the marvel that was Alani Lenika Hill. She was filled with nervous energy. Her leg bounced, and she leaned forward in her seat, anxiety filled. Worry had taken residence in her. "Are you okay?" she asked.

Ethic was full of tension. He had never been arrested, but he assumed that this was what sitting in a courtroom felt like, only Ethic was about to be judged by something greater than the law. He was preparing to go before God. Everything in him wanted to walk out, but if he did, she would as well. Only she would be walking away from him. She would leave. This was her only stipulation to stay. To get to know God. To commune with his Father, but Ethic was a child, abandoned, and he harbored some resentments. It would not be an easy reunion. Alani insisted, however. If he became acquainted, if he could scrape up even a little bit of faith, he could keep her. She would stay, and he would do anything to make her stay. He had never been so conflicted. War was being waged inside of him. Utter turmoil wrecked his soul; but for her, he remained unmoved on the outside. He nodded.

"I'm good, baby." His voice was deep. Sturdy. Sure. It was strong because he knew it was the version of himself that she needed in this moment. It wasn't what he felt, but it was what she required, and he wasn't in a position to ever be less than she needed. He wouldn't be able to fall short with her - ever. He had already done the worst. He could only contribute to her growth. Any action that negated that would be met with her evacuation. She would pull out on him and Ethic couldn't let that happen. He had to be perfect. For her. The love she gave him was, so he had to meet her at her standard. Motherfucking perfection. Her misted eyes held so much uncertainty. So much fear. He knew she was taking a gamble on him. She was fighting so many things, just to allow herself to love him, and he was grateful because he knew he was undeserving of her. He reached for her hand, and for the first time in a long time, she didn't recoil. Her participation felt like a gift. His chest swelled, as she leaned into him and she placed those pouted lips on his. Her left hand touched the side of his face and he wanted to bitch up. She was back. Alani, not Lenika, had returned to him. He rested his forehead against hers and she moved her lips to his cheek, and then rested her cheek against the place she had left a lipstick stain. Cheek to cheek, as she wrapped four fingers behind his neck, her thumb caressing the lobe of his ear. She was touching him with such tenderness.

"I'm scared," she whispered.

A tender spot formed right behind his gunshot wound because he was fearful too. Afraid of failing her. Terrified to lose her. Petrified to face Him. Horrified of the possibility that even with God in the middle, they still may not make it. He spoke none of these insecurities, however. If she was weak, he had to stand tall. He had to be brave for them both. He had to have faith. Alani spoke about it like it was so simple…like she could just arm herself with it and go out into the world to slay the obstacles of her day. Ethic knew nothing about the spiritual warfare that surrounded him every second of everyday. The angels and demons fighting over the outcome of his life. A war over his soul. God versus the devil, since the day he was born. Alani was forcing him to arm himself and to choose a side, to get to know the word of God and to slay those demons that had tortured him. Alani was his prayers manifested. That much he knew to be true. He pulled back to stare into her glossy eyes.

"I love you."

She pulled air into her lungs; long, deep, centered, conscious breathing. She was absorbing his energy. He had spoken it into the universe, manifesting a palpable feeling so strong that she could almost see it, as it lingered between them. She inhaled, absorbing it…his love.

"I have been in love with you since the day I met you. There hasn't been a second when I couldn't feel it. There won't ever be a moment when I don't feel it," she whispered. "I know she left you. Your mother. I won't. Not again. I'll be everything for you, Ethic. A friend, a mother, a lover, a spiritual anchor. I got lost for a minute, but I'm here now. I'll be all that and I only need you to be one thing," she whispered.

"What's that?" he asked.

"Godly," she replied.

He nodded, and his face contorted in pain. It hurt so badly. The thought of transformation. The process of becoming that for her. It was like a burn, not easily cured, not quickly calmed. It scorched until it didn't and every second until it was healed was felt. There was no speeding up the process. He nodded, again, trying to encourage himself. He could do this, maybe not by himself, but with her at his side he could do it...he could do this and much more. With her, he could fly, so why couldn't he drop to his knees and submit to God? His eyes glossed over in turmoil. She caressed him.

"Just do this for me. Just try."

He sniffed away emotion, as he lowered his head. She cupped his face, lifting his chin. He was so broken. She had no idea how long he had waited for her; the things he had gone through; the L's he had taken.

"I'm good," he whispered, but his face contorted in devastation and he bit into his bottom lip to control the vibration of it. He was struggling. She could see it, and it broke her heart because he was normally so strong, so controlled... but when facing God, control was not his to maintain. Ethic had no wins in that bout. Conviction burned in him so fiercely that his skin was hot. She was pulling out the boy in him. The boy that needed guidance. She represented everything he had been lacking for so long. Mothers were the center of the black community. They nourished and guided and protected and educated and encouraged. He was so low on all of those things; and as he looked at Alani, he saw motherhood. He saw a God who could supply all that his mother had neglected to give him. He didn't believe in God, but he did believe in her, so maybe she was his God. *In His image and all that,* Ethic thought. Perhaps, women, all of them, mothers, daughters, who grew up to become mothers…women…the birthers…the creators…Alani Lenika Hill. Women were God.

He loved this woman. He loved her so very much.

"This will help us. Do you trust me?"

He nodded, and he meant it. He had never trusted anyone more.

The sound of the door to the church's office opening interrupted them.

"Alani, good to see you. Beautiful as always, baby girl."

Baby girl?

Ethic, instantly, pulled himself together. Alani was permitted to see his weakness. The outside world could never. He stood and extended his hand to the man in front of him. He was thrown by the man's informal appearance and his even more informal greeting to Alani. This wasn't the pastor that had spoken at the debutante pageant. This man was younger, comparable in age to him, dressed down in Jordan's and sweat pants, with a hoodie and a fitted cap that he wore to the back. They must have been making pastors in a new way these days because Ethic had never encountered one like this. He was built solid, like an athlete, and his kind eyes rounded out cocoa-colored skin. A goatee and thick, dark eyebrows contrasted against the color of his skin. Ethic was a confident man, but he couldn't help but wonder how much healing this pastor had put on Alani. He hadn't missed that this man called her Alani. Not Lenika. They were familiar with one another. They were more than familiar. Ethic shook his hand, tight grip, stern glower...un-fucking-friendly because he felt like he was in the presence of a man whom had fucked his woman before.

"Thank you for seeing us, Ny," Alani said. Alani hugged him, and Ethic felt a stir in his stomach. He was territorial. He had never been before, but this man, this pastor, was clearly connected to Alani's spirit. They had prayed together. They had communed together about God. That was something Ethic couldn't give her because he didn't believe. He felt threatened, like this man was the type of man that Alani needed.

"Anytime. I'm Nyair, man. I've heard a lot about you. Good to meet you, bruh."

"Ezra," Ethic answered. Ethic's brow was pinched in uncertainty. Alani had spoken to this man about him, but he knew nothing about Nyair.

Alani tucked herself under his arm and feathered Ethic's chin with the palm of her hand. He exhaled his unease. Her touch...just her touch...calmed his storm. She stood on her tip toes and kissed his lips, quick, but with need, pulling his bottom lip into her mouth.

"La told me you're new to all this. I think it would do us some good to take our first session outside. We can walk through the garden, talk a bit," Nyair said.

Ethic nodded, as Nyair led the way out the door. He was appreciative because the oxygen inside the church felt thick, like it was too good for sinners like him. He pulled in the unholy air as he stepped outside. Alani walked in the middle of them, as they crossed the parking lot and entered the groomed land behind the building. There were acres of vegetable fields that the church owned. A community garden where members came to feed their families.

"We started this garden five years ago. Corporations tried to come buy up the land behind the church. Wanted to build a strip mall. White people coming in buying up everything in the hood, pushing us out. I bought it and started planting. Forget the welfare, the public assistance. Mothers can come right here and pick what they need to feed the babies. We got to take care of our own, you know?" Nyair said. He bent to pick a tomato from the ground and tossed it to Alani. She caught it mid-air. "Remind me to send a basket home for Nannie. For that homemade pasta sauce she be whipping up."

Alani snickered. "You mean the sauce *I* be whipping up. Every time you ask for some, she makes me cook it!"

Nyair smiled.

"So, Ezra…"

"Ethic," he corrected. "You can call me Ethic."

"Ethic," Nyair said. "I've seen you around here, man. Baby girl, Bella, is your daughter, right?"

Ethic nodded. "My pride and joy."

"Must be hard, raising her alone. Alani tells me you have three children," Nyair added.

"We get by," Ethic answered. Alani noticed his guard. He was uncomfortable. She reached for his hand, wrapping her arm through his elbow, as she intertwined their fists. She gave him three squeezes. *I. Love. You.* Somehow, he knew what they meant, and he squeezed four times in return. *I. Love. You. Too.* With her urging him to open up, he added, "It is hard, sometimes, man. It feels impossible, some days."

"Those days are over," Alani whispered, pausing her step to turn to him. She wrapped her hand around his neck and kissed him, again.

"She loves you, man. I know she's struggled with that, but we've spoken a lot on forgiveness."

Ethic's brows lifted. He wasn't sure how much Nyair knew.

"For the lies. For hiding the parts of you that you knew I wouldn't accept," she clarified, easing him a bit.

"We always hide our worst parts. It's hard to confront them, not just in front of others, but in front of the mirror, you know? Can't show her because then you'll have to admit to yourself that part exists," Nyair said.

Ethic nodded. "I can face the reflection. It's getting someone else to accept the reflection that troubles me." He whispered it so low that it was barely audible. That confession of loneliness. The desertion. The inaptitude of being good enough for a mate, deserving of one, even. If his mother couldn't stomach him, how could he expect someone who had no responsibility to him to suffer through his presence?

"You would think it would be easier. Connection. Manifesting partnership with another. It should be. We come from connection. Born from it. Man and woman, connecting to reproduce that energy and reproduce themselves... creating children..."

"The connection would have to be true, in order to be replicated though, no?" Ethic responded. "Can't just plant seeds in anyone and then expect that seed to grow up and know something about love. A kid has to see that coming up. It has to be a part of his world. A visual lesson reinforced everyday by the people who created him, so that when he grows up, he knows how to seek that. If all he sees is disconnection, he becomes disconnected from love, from himself even."

Alani stood, baffled, as she looked at Ethic. He and Nyair were both speaking to her from the perspective of a black man. It was a depth of sensitivity she had never been blessed to witness in a man. Normally, black men were so hardened, so tough, almost afraid to be vulnerable. This complicated, eloquent exchange between two of the best men she knew was enlightening. She felt like a fly on the wall, like she was a spy for the female species...siphoning information to take back to explain the psyche of men. This was a rare occurrence. This spillage of secrets.

"You're absolutely right, bro. Train up a child in the way he should go and when he is old he will not depart from it," Nyair said.

"Proverbs?" Alani asked, frowning.

"You got the stank face because you've only heard the scripture referenced in one way. The Bible is a guide that we can interpret uniquely to match our experience. It isn't cut and dry the way a lot of old-school pastors would have us think. Train up a child is about more than habit, about more than chores, and teaching a kid to pray and obey. What about teaching love, showing love, modeling affection, being love in human form, so that when they grow up they are love in human form...they are God's love in human form? How amazing would it be if when you met this brother, he loved on you with God's love, with a love that was so second nature that it could never injure...never hurt? He wasn't trained up that way, so he's guessing. My G, you stumbling in the dark, trying to find her, trying to get it right but you're stubbing your toes along the way."

Ethic nodded.

"The heart of the father becomes the heart of the child, bruh," Nyair said. "If the man who raised you was heartless. If he loved you wrong, it's inevitable for you to love incorrectly."

"He loves perfectly," Alani defended. "I never said that, Ny."

"After making mistakes. That's correction, not perfection, Alani," Nyair said. "Why must you, or any woman he's chosen before you, have to suffer through correction, before reaching glorification? You shouldn't have to endure a storm first. That's not what love is about...putting up with hurt and being celebrated for staying through it."

That silenced her. Zipped her lips right on up and she pinched evil brows at him. She didn't want him to go this hard. This couldn't feel like an ambush or Ethic would never return. She needed Nyair to ease into this walk of faith, like a timid child going for a swim on a scolding day. If he pushed Ethic into the deep end, it would shock his system and hit him all at once. Ethic wasn't equipped to swim. He would drown. Their chance at fixing things would die.

"And you know about that, Ny," Alani challenged. "We're all flawed and just walking around trying to correct things we messed up before we were aware of the impact we made on others. It takes mistakes. It's what you learn from them... what I learn from them that matters."

She squeezed her fingers that were interlaced through Ethic's tighter. She was angry. She was defending him.

"You know I know better than anybody. Too many mistakes were made on my behalf. Ones that others suffered for. Ones that keep me up at night," Nyair said, his voice small, like it was hard to think about. Ethic observed his melancholy. He couldn't relate to his walk of faith, but he could relate to that...the somberness...the sorrow. He had made those type of mistakes. The ones that were so heavy he had to check out of reality sometimes within the confines of his basement. It was his retreat. Like the church was Alani's altar, his basement was where he unloaded his burdens. Yoga. The Zen. It wasn't prayer, but it helped. It helped quiet the conscience that haunted him. "The walls of this church don't take away regret. It just helps to manage it a bit. Gives me hope that I'm working toward being a better man," Nyair added.

"Hmm," Ethic gruffed, in deep thought.

"But look, man, I'm not gon' hold y'all all day. This is just an introduction. It was good to meet you. Alani, here, is persistent on scheduling something consistent, but I say just let it vibe," Nyair said. He pulled a card from his pants pocket and extended it to Ethic. "My perspective might not be for you. It might be different than what you believe. I'm always up for the conversation between gentlemen. We all just walking around, trying to figure it out, so I'm open, bro. Whenever you want to chop it up."

Ethic took the card and slid it into his pocket and then extended his hand. They shook.

"Good to know, my man. You have a good one," Ethic said.

"Yo, Alani. We're having dinner Sunday, after service. Zora's cooking up some wings for the game. Y'all should fall through," Nyair said.

"Yeah, we'll see," Alani nodded. "Thanks, Ny."

Nyair headed back toward the church and Alani rolled skeptical eyes up to Ethic.

He pulled her into his arms and she rested a cheek to his chest, wrapping her arms around his waist. Her heart was heavy, but there was no turning back. He exhaled, as he kissed the top of her head, and just the energy he transferred through that simple gesture filled her with courage. Courage to try. Will to make it.

"What now?" he asked.

"I don't know," she whispered. "I don't know."

CHAPTER 2

Morgan sat backstage, putting coconut oil all over her body.

"Your crew coming tonight?"

Mo looked in the reflection of the mirror at the white boy who stood behind her. White Boy Nick was nice on the dance floor. He put it down in the stilettos better than Mo.

"You know that nigga, Messiah, ain't missing a beat when it comes to Mo's ass," Aria said, from across the room, as she leaned close to the mirror to place her earrings in her ears. "Besides, you need him. You got to pull a guy out the crowd for the routine and you know he will burn this whole damn club down if you end up dancing on anybody else."

Mo chuckled.

"What about that fine-ass boy with the tattoos? Little light skinned. He can get it," Nick said.

Mo hollered in laughter, as she cut a side eye to Aria.

"You can get slapped too," Aria said.

"Oh, that's you? My bad, boo. I didn't know," Nick conceded.

Aria shook her head, as she applied her lipstick next. "Nope, that ain't me, but it's not gon' be you either. Ain't gon' be n'ann bitch up in this mu'fucka either. Little daddy in the Gucci and ink is off fucking limits," she got louder at the end, to let every dancer in the room know.

"How you know he gon' be in Gucci?" Morgan teased.

"Cuz the nigga's ghetto. All he know what to do with all that paper he got is buy Gucci shit," Aria said, smiling, as she shook her head.

Nick walked away, and Mo shook her head.

"For somebody that ain't feeling Isa, you sholl know a whole lot, sis," Morgan said, with a smirk.

"You worry about mean-ass Messiah," Aria said, with a snicker. "I've got Isa handled."

"Tell the truth. He popped that thang, didn't he?" Morgan whispered.

If Aria's skin wasn't so rich, she would have blushed. Her eyes sparkled, as she shook her head. "If he ever pop this, you'll know. The nigga entire steelo would switch up. I'm talking nose wide open, picking me up, dropping me off, bringing me food, buying me shit, trying to be all up under me. I don't need Isa smothering my ass. I'm wild and free. I'ma die wild and free. He can't handle it. I'd fuck his entire world up, if I ever let him dip in it."

Morgan chuckled and stood to her feet. She wore black, dancer's bikini bottoms with ripped fishnet stockings beneath. Her high-heeled Timberland construction wheats were good and broken in. She had been walking around in them for weeks. The cropped, mini, Champion hoodie she wore showed her belly and she sucked in her stomach.

"Bitch, am I getting fat?" Morgan asked, as she turned to

the side, frowning, and then admired her reflection from the back. Her hips and behind had definitely spread and she wasn't as toned as she would like.

"That's Messiah doing all that damage," Aria snickered, with raised brows. "All y'all do is eat and fuck. Can't pay y'all to go on a real date."

"We date! We just not dating with you and Isa. You just want an excuse to go out with him without having to give in when he asks," Morgan laughed.

"Whatever!" Aria smiled. "We're up. You ready?"

Morgan followed Aria to the edge of the stage. "Did you tell Messiah and the crew to sit at the tables up front?"

"I told him, and I put the manager up on game," Morgan confirmed.

Aria went out on stage.

"Yo, Detroit!!!" she shouted, as she clicked on the mic and switched out onto the stage.

The crowd went crazy. Morgan closed her eyes, taking in the applause, as she stood off to the side.

"Who's ready for Stiletto Gang?!?"

The applause and catcalls rang out. Stiletto Gang's popularity was growing by the day. Morgan was up to a million followers on Instagram and Aria had danced for numerous artists, including a Coachella performance with one of the largest artists in the world. They were young, beautiful, and talented. They went from city to city, booking gigs at local clubs and they always sold out. Morgan was barely balancing the last few weeks of school, with all the appearances they were securing.

"Who y'all excited to see? Y'all ready for Mo Money?" Aria hyped. The deaf dancer. The crowd erupted, and Morgan felt the energy take over her body. Nerves rattled throughout her, but she knew as soon as the music began, and she zoned out, they would disappear. "Show us some love, everybody!"

Morgan walked out onto the stage with three other dancers. White Boy Nick was another favorite because he didn't always join them, but when he did, the LGBT community came out in the masses to support.

Morgan's eyes instantly found Messiah. He sat in the crowd, wearing all black, dressed down, because she knew he had cut his business short to show up and that he would be heading directly back to it once he'd shown his support. Meek and Isa rounded out the crew, per usual. Their entire table was silent, and Morgan smirked because she could tell they were slightly uncomfortable. Flint niggas. Hood niggas. In Detroit, out of their element, and undoubtedly strapped in case anything popped off. Morgan wouldn't be surprised if another car full of goons were posted in the parking lot. Precautions. Messiah leaned back in his chair, shot her a wink, so she knew that his eyes were on her, and rubbed his hands together before throwing one arm over the back of his chair. His legs spread wide, arrogantly, confidently, like he knew he had both the biggest dick and gun in the room. Morgan knew both to be true. Morgan closed her eyes and then the beat dropped. Kanye West.

Yeah, you supermodel thick
Damn, that ass bustin' out the bottom
I'ma lose my mind in it, crazy that medulla oblongata

Morgan lost her mind in the song, as she went into a full twerk, while White Boy Nick danced behind her. Her personality on stage always made her stand out. She bit that tongue, through an arrogant smirk, as she rolled her body to the beat and then slid down to one knee. Nick hyped her up, dancing to an eight count behind her. She lifted her leg straight up in the air and Nick pushed it down, sending her into a full split. In her mind, Messiah was under that split and she worked him. She rolled to her feet and her midsection might as well have been disconnected from her body the way she moved it but nothing else. The DJ mixed in a song, slowing it down, and Morgan and Aria made their way over to Messiah's table. Messiah shifted in discomfort. Morgan smiled at his unease. He shook his head as Morgan approached, strutting to the seductive beat of Ella Mai, only her tip toes gracing the floor. Aria grabbed Isa's hand and pulled him up to the stage where two chairs now sat. Morgan attempted to grab Messiah, but he shook his head and she was sure she saw a blush as he smiled, relaxing for the first time. Center of attention wasn't his thing. No way was he getting up on that stage.

Messiah turned to Meek and nodded toward the stage.

"Yo, bro, save me. You know this ain't my scene," he said.

Morgan pouted but accepted Meek as a consolation prize, grabbing his hand and leading him back to the stage.

The crowd went crazy, as Morgan and Aria circled their prey, as the DJ played the lyrics.

I know you're on your way
To get caught up in the way
We turnin' night into mornin'
I keep you up, keep it goin'
Make you feel a way
Yeah, I'm gon' have my way
So tell me I get it, I own it
Own it, own it, own it
Ooh yeah, ooh yeah

Morgan straddled Meek, sinking slowly into his lap, as she gripped the sides of his face, staring directly in his eyes, lips inches from his, as she hit a seductive grind. Meek lifted hands of surrender and the crowd went wild, as Morgan rolled in his lap. This was more than dancing; this was sex, this was dry humping, if the barrier of their clothes didn't exist, they would be fucking. It had been planned that way because she had thought Messiah would be beneath her. Mo tried to keep it as tasteful as possible, but the dance was just too erotic. No matter what she did, she would excite him. She felt it and her heart fluttered in her chest. She was a woman and he was a man, so her body betrayed her as the seat of her panties dewed. Mo was wet.

"Oh my god," Isa was loud enough to make the crowd ignite. Morgan glanced to her left, but she didn't need to. She already knew that Aria was working Isa over because... well, that had been the plan. Every man in the crowd wished they could somehow switch places with the men on stage. Morgan stood on heeled feet, then placed one foot on the edge of the chair. She was grateful the grinding was over but now her sex was in his face, on his lips. He could smell it, she knew he could because he bit his bottom lip. If it were Messiah sitting there, he would have kissed it.

I'ma let you play with this
Play that shit, stay in it, uh, huh
Just tell me you want it

She rolled her pussy in Meek's face and smiled, arrogantly, biting her tongue, as he blew out a breath. She had him stressed. She could see it. He was holding his breath and trying hard not to react, but the tension in those lines in his forehead told her he was bothered. She grabbed his head and rolled his neck forward, as she twerked.

And I know you love the taste of it
Take a whole damn plate of it
Baby, save that shit

She released him and circled the chair, as Aria did the matching eight count on Isa. They strutted behind the fellas and leaned over them, rubbing their hands down their chests before walking around to the front and standing in front of them.

Own it, own it, own it

Morgan and Aria ended in freestyles and Morgan took off. In her zone, all she heard were the other dancers as they came back onto the stage.

"Aye!! Bitch! Go. The. Fuck. Off!" Aria clapped her hands with every word.

The DJ mixed in another track and Kendrick Lamar turned her up a notch.

I said I'm geeked and I'm fired up.

Aria and the other dancers joined in and they did a quick 16 counts. Morgan threw up two M's and bit her bottom lip, as her face curled up, hitting a sexy variation of a Crip walk, before lifting her leg lazily, doing a stripper swag walk, as she alternated from heel to heel.

Loyalty, loyalty, loyalty.
Tell me who you loyal to?

The music ended, and Morgan could barely breathe, as the DJ shouted, "Stiletto motherfucking Gang, everybody. Give it up." The crowd gave up everything, rocking the club so hard that Aria kept dancing. Morgan was covered in sweat and heaving. Her gaze found Messiah and her smile melted from her face. He was bothered. She could see it. The tension in his shoulders were like bricks and his stare was like a beam on a gun. He was ready for a kill shot. Her heart skipped a beat, as she watched him lean onto his knees and rub those two fingers together. Morgan pointed to her face and used her pointer fingers to draw a smile on her face.

"Smile," she mouthed to him. "I love you."

He read her lips and flicked his nose, shaking his head, as he rubbed his temples with one hand, in distress. Meek and Isa made their way back over to the table and slapped hands with Messiah. Morgan noticed Messiah pull Meek in with extra aggression, then whisper something in his ear. Morgan's gut hollowed until she saw the smile melt on both their faces, as they clowned over an apparent inside joke. *Probably a death threat*, Morgan thought. Morgan made her way off the stage, with Aria not far behind. She walked up on Messiah and straight into his arms, weaseling her way underneath his right arm.

"Yo, I'm not coming to no more of this shit, shorty. Fuck that," he whispered.

"Bet you next time you'll come on stage instead of sending your homeboy," she teased.

He snickered, releasing a stubborn half smirk. "I swear to God I want to break that nigga jaw right now. He lucky he controlled his hands. That sight don't belong in my head. You can't do that shit to me, Mo. Moving that shit like that. Pussy all in a nigga face, ass all in his lap. I swear to God, you want to send me to jail." He shook his head and Morgan laughed, as she kissed him. He was stubborn and bothered, so he pulled back, but Morgan grabbed his chin.

"Don't play," she snapped, her long stiletto nails curving around his face. He was angry. She could feel the heat coming from him. The sex later would be amazing, heightened, because she knew he would try to punish her. He gave her a rough kiss and pulled back, but Morgan finessed his chin back to her, gripping tightly, sternly. "Stop. Playing. With. Me. You know I'll show out in here on your ass. These my lips or has something changed?"

21

He looked away and she pulled him right back.

"You already know," he gave up.

"Then act like it," she said, as she fed him her tongue. Morgan kissed him so deeply that she felt his dick brick against her. Morgan inhaled him like he was oxygen...like she had been deprived and was finally able to breathe. Messiah placed hands around her waist and then slid them down, cupping the bottom of her ass, squeezing, then pulling her into him. He was ready to fuck. She was game for whatever. Weed and cognac lived on his tongue. It made sense because she was high and drunk...off him...Morgan stayed in outer space when he was around. He lifted her, made her body feel like it was vibrating. Messiah was a drug, all by himself, and Morgan Atkins was addicted. He had her head gone and there was no recovery.

"Gang! Gang! Gang! Gang!"

Morgan turned back toward the stage and the crowd was hype, chanting, demanding that they return to the stage.

She turned to Aria who shrugged and headed back to the stage. The girl was built for the spotlight and it posed a dilemma to Messiah because he found comfort in the shadows.

The DJ dropped Cardi through the speakers.

"Oh, he want me to cut the fuck up out here," Aria snickered. "You leading or you want me to make up the count?"

"You can," Morgan said. She wasn't really looking forward to another set because she knew she was pushing it. Messiah was already tight about the lap dance. He was in his feelings and she didn't want to push her luck, but she was already on the stage.

That ass, that ass, that ass, that ass...
She bad, she bad, she bad, she bad...

Leave it up to Aria to throw that thang in a circle like a stripper, and then open her arms wide like she was up for a challenge. Morgan looked at Messiah, who was already disinterested. She saw him blow air from his mouth, as he leaned over to Isa. She froze. She shook her head and cut her hand across her neck.

"I'm good," she said.

"Mo Money, the crowd love you, baby. Shine, baby girl," the DJ called out over the mic, putting her on the spot.

"Mo! Mo! Mo! Mo!" the crowd joined in and Morgan cut eyes back to Messiah. His brows lifted in wonder, as he shook his head. Those trigger fingers rubbing, her heart racing...

"Let's give the superstar her own track!" The DJ shouted. Morgan extended her hand, shaking it and her head to decline.

THEN THE FUCKING BEAT DROPPED.

Cash Money Records taking over for the '99 and the 2000's

"Oh, bitch, you betta!" Aria shouted.
Fuck it.
Nobody twerked like Mo. She was the queen at it. You would think she earned a living off that ass...she could earn

a living off that ass. The best stripper couldn't keep up. Her arms rose in the air, she turned her ass to the crowd and clicked on, hearing nothing, feeling nothing, but the beat to the music.

You can do a trick, yeah, on the dick, yeah.

Morgan brought one leg up to her ear in a standing split on that lyric. Her bikini was so tiny that it rolled up her voluptuous behind, wedging in the crack of her ass like a thong. Morgan Atkins had ass everywhere. She walked her fingers up that leg, and then brought it down, putting hands to knees as Aria geeked her.

Aria came up behind her and got eye level with Morgan's recently-gained weight, pretending like she was smacking it. Then, Aria joined in. The whole club went psycho, as the other dancers came on the stage as hype men. By the time the song went off, there was money on the stage, a few thousand dollars, if Mo had to guess.

Wobble dee, wobble dee, wob-wobble dee, wobble dee
Drop, drop it like it's hot.

The duo was selling straight ratchetness and sex, but they were having the time of their lives. They laughed, making stank faces, because they knew when they were on point. Aria and Mo had a short hand with one another like a team of surgeons. They just danced well together and tonight they were raping the stage. It felt like the best night of their lives and they were all smiles. They had turned the club into a strip

24

joint, there was so much money flying at them. When the song finally went off, the DJ shouted, "Mo Money, everybody. Give it up for Stiletto Gang. Gang…Gang…Gang…"

The chant continued, as the crowd joined in and Morgan and Aria hugged, while smiling, as they made their way backstage. As soon as Morgan opened the door to their changing room, she saw Messiah, leaning against the vanity where she dressed.

She stopped dead in her tracks.

"Let me go find me some business," Aria said, as she backpedaled out of the room. Morgan closed and locked the door.

She couldn't gauge his temperature, but his stare was deadly and those fucking fingers. They were going.

"Ssiah…"

"Get over here, Mo. Why the fuck you all the way across the room?" he asked.

She sighed and walked into his space. Messiah stepped to the side and turned around, so that he was standing behind her. He kissed the back of her neck and bent her over the vanity.

Before she could even speak, she felt rough hands pulling her bottoms down and he was inside her. Morgan moaned in approval. He was angry, so he wasn't gentle. He pulled her hair, using it as his reigns as he beat up the box, driving her crazy.

"Damn, this shit sooo fucking wet. Who you wet for, shorty?" A flash of guilt flooded her because she had felt her panties soak during the lap dance, but it was innocent, it was just a dance, and Messiah was her man. He had sent his friend up there…she only wanted him. Messiah was all she ever wanted, and she needed him…needed this…*God, just like fucking this*…all the time.

"You," she whispered, as she threw it back on him like she was still on the stage…like it was still 1999. "Yes! Ssiah!"

He ran one hand down her sweaty back and then gripped her hips, pulling her into him. He split her in half, as he admired the work he made of her body. His black dividing her pink. Her wetness covering him. Her tightness pulling him. The visual was always the best part. Her sex gripped him, as she slid on and off, again and again and he bit into his lower lip.

"Messiah, baby, I'm there," she whimpered, as she placed hands on the mirror in front of her. They were knocking all types of makeup and lotion to the floor. Neither cared.

"Me too, baby; damn, me too." Her face twisted, and he grunted, as he dug into her depths, leaving his seeds inside before he pulled out. She turned to him and sat on the vanity, as she kissed his lips.

"You keep showing out and you gon' get a nigga hurt," Messiah said, while shaking his head in disdain. "That shit be eating me up, shorty. You don't even know." He snickered. "Fucking throwing money on the stage. I would have snatched your ass off that bitch, if you bent down to touch one dollar."

Morgan laughed and kissed him, again. "I'ma hate Juvenile forever after watching that shit," he mumbled. She planted her head in his chest and hollered in amusement.

"Yo, shorty, you fucking got it. No lie. I just wanted to taste that shit, so I know every other nigga in this club want to eat off my plate. You know what happens when you try to take a bone off a dog plate?"

She nodded.

"It bites…"

"Exactly, shorty," Messiah said. He tapped her nose and then grabbed her hand to lead her out the club.

CHAPTER 3

Morgan was a beauty. She knew it. She had always known it. It was the first thing people said when they saw her. Ever since she was little. "Aww… she's so pretty." It was a compliment she had received many times. She would read the lips of her mother's friends, when she was younger, and they would say exactly that. She was Justine Atkins' walking baby doll, and because she had grown up deaf they treated her as such. She had been handled with kid gloves her entire life, until meeting Messiah. He handled her roughly. He flipped and fucked her little ass in every direction, without care that she was fragile. With him, she wasn't delicate at all. She was strong. She was sharp. She was everything other than what people expected her to be. She loved the identity he gave her… the fearlessness…the feeling of importance…like she was priority number one and everything else in his life came behind her. Only after she was pleased 100 percent would Messiah leave her side, and if she beckoned, he came right back. Morgan stepped out of the shower and wrapped her towel around her body and then looked at herself in the mirror. Something was different. She felt it. She had been feeling it for weeks, but the too little clothes, the random nausea that hit her sometimes out of the blue... *I didn't miss my cycle, though*, she thought. She reached for her purse and pulled the pregnancy test from inside. She had made an excuse to stop by the local pharmacy on the way to Messiah's place. Morgan had an overwhelming inkling that she might be pregnant. She hadn't even told Messiah her suspicions because she didn't want to get his hopes up if it was a false alarm. Morgan was in love and as she held the pregnancy test in her hands, she hoped it came back positive. She was an 18-year-old girl. Her first year of college was nearing its end. The world was at her feet. A baby should have been the last thing on her mind, but she desperately wanted it. She needed something secure...something that would guarantee that Messiah would never leave her life. He wanted it too, so it wasn't a trap. It was a plan...their plan, and as the seconds ticked by, Morgan felt desperation sneaking up her spine. When had two minutes become so damn long? It was 120 seconds of pure torture.

She looked at the stick and her stomach clenched, filling with anxiety. Two pink lines appeared on the screen and Morgan's legs weakened. A hollowness filled her, as she brought one hand to her mouth in excitement, jumping up and down in silent celebration. Her eyes filled with tears. She was pregnant. Filled with Messiah. Growing not just any baby but *his* baby inside her. She would finally have a family of her own that no one could take away. She felt like crying, but she couldn't. She wouldn't tell him now, not tonight. It was a bad time to spring something so distracting on him, so she would hold it. For now. Morgan wanted some time to wrap her mind around it anyway. She needed this. She was growing wearier by the day, afraid that Ethic would find out about her affair with Messiah. This baby would force Ethic's hand. Messiah would have to be around, and Ethic would just have to accept it. She was sure there would be static, initially, but Ethic was all about family. No way would he keep up the animosity with his grandchild on the way. She put the stick back in the box and hid it under the sink, all the way toward the back, before washing her hands and emerging. Nervous energy pulsed through her. Just the revelation that she was housing life inside her made her feel dizzy. Adulation swarmed her. This was confirmation. She and Messiah would be connected, through blood, through love, forever…they had created forever. To two people who had felt nothing but inconsistency their entire lives, the gift of being connected for a lifetime was worth more than gold. They had bottled up a moment in time and planted it inside Morgan, so even when the moment passed, they would have physical evidence that it had existed…evidence in human form that she had loved a god once and his name was Messiah. She opened her towel and looked at her belly. She seemed to be gaining weight everywhere except her stomach. She was wide; hips and ass were spilling everywhere. Morgan had always been on the slimmer side but indulging in Messiah had added a few pounds to her physique. She was sure the baby had added on 10 more because she was vixen thick. The dancing ensured it settled on her frame just right, but she couldn't believe she hadn't noticed it before. No wonder Messiah couldn't leave her alone. He had been all over her, lately. She found him standing in his bedroom fully dressed. Black jeans, black hoodie, underneath a black, leather jacket. Her heart sank. She knew what night it was, and she hated it. Every Thursday it was the same. He robbed a semi-truck and Morgan would be up all night, with knots of tension in her stomach, worrying. Friday and Saturday, he would distribute product, the rest of the week was hers. She wanted more. She needed him 24/7, safe in her arms, warm in their bed. Yes, theirs because she had practically moved in.

Messiah paused to look up at her. He always took the time to gather a mental snapshot of her in his head, just in case he didn't make it back. He wanted to be able to remember what she looked like, every detail, so that he could play it in his mind before he died, if, God forbid, someone caught him slipping. He loved her. Never did he think he was even capable of the emotion, but for her, it was present, and he was tired of hiding.

"It's time to tell Ethic," Messiah whispered.

"It is not time to tell Ethic," Morgan defied, shaking her head, knowing that the revelation of their illicit affair had to be planned. It wasn't something they could just pull up and admit to. Morgan wanted to be further along in her pregnancy and showing some. They needed all the leverage they could get. Keeping something like this from Ethic was betrayal. The reveal would burn him. He would be upset about her having a baby so young, but he loved her, he loved Messiah too. He would come around, but Morgan wanted to make sure the notion of an abortion was off the table.

"I'm a grown-ass man, Mo. I can't keep sneaking. You're

practically living here now. I need to have a conversation with him about a few things, in fact. I fucked up. It's some things he needs to know. Some things I've got to get off my chest. I don't know how the cards will fall after that conversation, but I can't keep avoiding it."

He walked over to her and sat on the bed, pulling her into his lap.

"I know Ethic. He won't be happy about this. He lost my sister so violently."

Messiah captured her chin between his fingers, lifting it slightly, steadying her invisible crown because he'd be damned if it ever fell. He stared her in the eyes and Morgan could feel his love. It spread through her every time their gaze connected. "You're not your sister. I know you pride yourself in being like her. Raven Atkins was the princess of the city. Pretty, spoiled, but you're not her, Mo. You're the queen, shorty. You don't chase after the nigga that call the shots, you give the nigga shots. You tell me when to move, how to move. You the general, Mo. You got a fucking killer on your team. What we have is nothing like anything your sister went through. It's different. You're different," Messiah stated.

"She's all he'll see when he looks at us, though, baby. He looks at me and he sees Rae. I need him to be okay with this, Messiah; and if that's ever going to happen, I want to prove to him that we're different...that you're different. That requires some changes."

He craned his neck back, so that they weren't so close... so that he could look her in the eyes. Curiosity pushed his brows up.

"Have you ever thought about leaving the streets?" she asked.

Messiah shook his head. "The streets raised me, Mo. That's like asking a nigga to leave his mama alone. They brought me up. They fed me. I can't. It's all I know," he said. "It's all I've got."

"Not anymore," she whispered, as she rubbed the back of his neck. "You have me, and I have you. I want us to last. I want us to do this right. I need you to think about what's next."

"Next?" he asked. This felt like pressure. This felt like the talk women gave men they had been involved with for years. The ultimatum that came when a ring was long overdue, or a job had been scarce for too long, or one too many fuck-ups had occurred. This was a stipulation. No matter how nice Morgan tried to make it sound, she was telling him he had to change something in order to keep her. She was elevating, and if he remained in the same place, he would lose her. He knew the day would come. Morgan Atkins was royalty, of course her expectations would be high. She was growing, and she was forcing him to level up as well.

"What comes after the drugs and the heists, Messiah? What is it that you want to do that will guarantee that you come home to me every night?" she asked. "If we go to Ethic and tell him about us, he will disapprove, as long as you're in the streets."

"That nigga made millions in the same game. He's the last person that can judge," Messiah said.

"Yeah, and his bank account is full, but his life is empty. It cost him everything. Just think about it, okay?" Morgan asked, as she brought her lips to his. "You're brilliant. You're running a business... it's illegal, but it's still a business and you're good at it. There's no reason why you can't do it in the real world, in a suit and tie, with a wife and a kid waiting at home for you. The safe way. The way Ethic will approve of."

"I put all the bad in you and you put all the good in me," Messiah whispered. "Doesn't feel like a fair exchange, Mo. You're too good for me, shorty. The best thing that ever happened in my whole, fucked-up life."

"Will you think about it?" she asked.

He nodded. "We'll talk about it when I get back." He kissed her and then lifted her from his lap.

"Don't wait up for me," Messiah said, as he went into his closet, hitting the numbers on the electronic safe that lay inside. It beeped open and Messiah retrieved three pistols. Two, he put in shoulder holsters. One, he handed to her. He insisted that she sleep with it on the nightstand on nights like these. Just in case.

"I don't want you to do this," she whispered.

"Shorty, we can't go through this every time," he said. He stood in front of her and swept her messy hair from her face.

"When is enough, enough? You have money, Messiah. More than enough to live off of for years. I hate this. I never close my eyes when you leave here on Thursdays. It's my least favorite day, and it used to be my favorite because Shondaland comes on, on Thursdays, and you're fucking it all up!" She whined. "Can't even concentrate because I'm sick, thinking about what I would do if something happened to you."

"What did I tell you? Huh? I got a reason to make it home now. Before you, I would take extra risks, go too hard for the bag and not even really give a fuck if I lived to spend the shit. That's different now. Everything's changed because I know you're here, waiting for me, and if I don't walk back through the door it's going to ruin you. I'd never do that to you. I'm always coming home to you, Mo."

She nodded. She had so much to say, but she couldn't put it on his heart before sending him out into the world. She needed him focused. She needed his heart black and cold, so he could live for her to thaw it another day. He gazed at her for a long time and then lifted her right hand, the one she wore his ring on. He brought it to his lips. "Enjoy Shondaland, shorty. Don't get too wrapped up in Dr. McDreamy, you know a nigga get jealous and shit." A smirk covered his face, as he kissed her ring finger and then he left her standing alone, as he headed out into the night.

Morgan sat in Messiah's bed, remote control in her hand, and a bowl of ice cream in her lap. The TV watched her because Morgan couldn't focus. It should have been a normal night but there was a nagging deep down in her soul. She was about to have a baby and Messiah was in the streets heavy. It bothered her because raising her child without a father was not an option. She knew what that felt like and no way would she want that for her baby. She had lost a lot to the streets; Messiah wouldn't be another. She hoped the fact that she was about to bring life into the world would be enough for him to hang up his hustle and legitimize things. Her favorite shows played in front of her, but she missed every single detail. Her head was spinning with possibility. Her life was about to change. She was about to receive a love that would never leave, and Morgan felt relieved because since the day her father died, love had seemed fleeting. It had felt like Ethic would wake up one day and decide that he no longer owed her father a debt and would take his love away. Like he loved her out of obligation, instead of naturally. Even Messiah's love could expire. She'd had to beg him for it in the first place. The love of her child's would never. Morgan had been chasing permanency for a long time. Everything always came off temporary. That love wasn't contrived or agreed upon between individuals, it was as natural as the birds that accompanied the rising of the sun on a summer day. Bond between mother and child was an element, like water, it replenished the weariest of souls and Morgan's was in need of Agape love. To have something solid, something real; a child of her own was miraculous. She finally had foundation. Something grounded to keep her rooted. She had a reason to make something of herself because now a little life was depending on her. She couldn't wait until Messiah made it home. Sharing the news with him would relieve a bit of the anxiety she felt. Carrying a secret this huge was eating her alive. She was too overjoyed. It felt like a current of electricity was pulsing throughout her entire body. It was orgasmic, like when Messiah was inside her, because technically, he was still inside her. He had put something there that would live, a piece of him, the best parts of him grew there, in her soil. Morgan had to do all she could to reap a good harvest… to birth a healthy baby. Morgan was loving a man that had never been loved properly a day in his life. It was difficult, sometimes. He resisted her, sometimes, often preparing her for an inevitable split that he seemed to be anticipating. She knew Messiah felt unworthy of her. She hoped giving him a family, a baby, helped ease his insecurity. She wasn't going anywhere. No matter what. She was committed to riding out the storm. Dedicated to finding comfort in his rough edges. Loyal to his brokenness because she was broken too, and somehow, two broken people had become a remedy for one another. She wished she could call her mother. It wasn't often that she thought of Justine Atkins. She had been a daddy's girl; but today, on a day when fear was lacing joy and she questioned if she was good enough to raise a child of her own, she needed motherly guidance. She desperately wanted words of affirmation to encourage her. The idea of pushing something out of her vagina, of being responsible for an entire breathing being, of the hard days of pregnancy ahead. It all had her terrified. Morgan was ecstatic to do this for Messiah, to give this to Messiah, but the not knowing of it all, the anxiety over the way her body would change, her life would evolve, had her shook. She was only 18. Would she be able to finish college? What about dancing? Was she giving up her life too soon? So many plaguing thoughts ran through her mind in that bed.

Morgan kicked the covers off her body and climbed from the bed, grabbing a pillow and taking it to the mirror. She lifted her shirt. Well... his shirt but, it was hers by default because she slept in it every night she was forced to be away from him. She stuffed it underneath her shirt and frowned, as she turned to the side.

"Pregnant," Morgan whispered, in disbelief. "I can pull off pregnancy. I'll dance every day, so I won't get fat. I'll take my vitamins, I'll put cocoa butter on every day, so I won't get stretch marks. I'll tell Ethic when it's too late for him to do anything about it...I'll get Messiah out of the streets and everything will be fine. Everything will work out. This baby won't change us. He'll love me more and we'll be a family."

But what if he loves me less? What if what we have turns into something else and we become those people who love their kid, but hate the person they made it with?

The sound of the doorbell ringing throughout the home, interrupted Morgan's thoughts and she snatched the pillow from beneath her shirt, dropping it to the floor. She frowned, then carried hurried feet to the bedroom window and noticed a car parked in the driveway. She reached for the gun on the nightstand, before heading downstairs. She thought about calling Messiah. No one knew where he lived, so a random visitor at 3:00 a.m. should never occur, but Morgan didn't want to bother him. She didn't want to distract him from the task of unloading the semis. One little misstep could end up with Messiah dead. His head needed to be in the game, not on her, not on this pop-up. Morgan would have to handle whomever it was herself. The gun in her hand eased her worries a bit. The chime of the bell went off, again, this time signaling impatience because whomever it was pressed the button three times. Irritation played with Morgan, as she traveled to the door. She peeked through the blinds to find a girl standing there, holding a sleeping baby on her shoulder.

"Who the fuck…"

She pulled open the door, confusion wearing her and irritation dancing in her eyes. The only thing that even urged her to unlock the door was the child in the girl's arms.

"Can I help you?" she asked.

The girl snickered and pushed into the home, passing Morgan like she owned the place. She looked at the open door and the darkness of the outside, and then her eyes rolled back to this girl…this storm that had swept suddenly into her night. She had a feeling this girl was about to destroy some things…a category five…yep, this girl had come to blow shit down.

"Messiah!"

Morgan recoiled, snapping her neck back, flabbergasted at the audacity of it all.

"Umm, bitch, I will beat your whole ass, baby in your arms and all. Who are you? And why are you knocking on my man's door at 3:00 a…the fuck…m?" Morgan's grip tightened on the gun, as she eased the safety off.

The girl scoffed, curling her lip up into a condescending smile. "You must be the bitch he's fucking. The one that has his head fucked up…"

"Nah, I'm the bitch he's loving. The one that put his tongue to work because I stay sitting on that nigga face. Who are you? Last time I'm going to ask," Morgan said, as she raised the gun.

Intuition told her she didn't want to know the answer to that question. The answer had the potential to tear her apart. She could feel it coming. She could feel her life in flux, anticipating the change that the presence of this stranger was about to deliver. Morgan tensed. Her entire body, from her trigger finger to her bowels, to her toes, to her heart...even the hairs on the back of her neck stood tall because a woman just knew when shit was about to go wrong. She was already angry at Messiah and she hadn't even heard what was about to roll off this girl's tongue yet.

I'm slapping fire from his ass. Her ass too. Whole toddler about to be on the floor. Fuck that baby. God, is this his baby?

Morgan was doing the math in her head, estimating, adding, subtracting, dividing, common core, algebra, shit... calculating in every fathomable way trying to determine when and how this little boy had come to be. He looked old enough to be before her, but it didn't matter...jealousy, unlike anything Morgan had ever felt, burned her. Morgan wasn't a fool, even if this child was made before her, the gall of this woman coming to his house, causing static in the middle of the night had to mean something. *He's still fucking her,* Morgan assumed. Messiah was tried and convicted in the court of Morgan and he didn't even know anything was going down. She felt sick, short of breath, dizzy. Was it her baby? *God, I'm pregnant with his baby and he's fucking with someone else.* The thought made her lose strength in her legs, but she didn't fold, wouldn't fold, not in front of this bitch.

"You laying in here, sitting in this bitch like you the queen. Did he tell you about his family? Bet his ass ain't tell you that!"

"Messiah!" The girl barked. The baby in her arms whined and the girl bounced him, to no avail. The little boy woke up, crying, and when he turned to Morgan she was gutted. He was Messiah's twin, down to the locs and brooding eyes.

Morgan's face didn't reveal her dismay, but her insides disintegrated, started at her head and crashing to her feet, like two planes had collided with her tower of love. 9/11. A national tragedy. The sight of this little boy leveled her.

"He's not here," Morgan whispered. "You need to leave."

"No, bitch, you need to leave. You don't belong here. He got your ass living up in here. I could fucking kill his stupid-ass," the girl snapped.

Morgan felt dazed, like the girl had slapped her. She wanted to fight. She wanted to kill somebody, but she knew this girl was just the messenger. Messiah's deceit had given this girl leverage, like the girl at the skating rink. Another woman knew something about her man that Messiah had neglected to divulge.

Don't press green on this bitch. Don't slap her. Don't fuck this bitch and her ugly-ass baby up, Morgan thought. It burned her that the little boy was adorable. She had to remind herself that the offender was Messiah. She wanted to body Messiah Williams, baby-daddy-to-be, ex-boyfriend-to-be, dead-ass-nigga-to-be, because Morgan was already making plans for murder.

"You let Messiah know he can't hide his family. It's a wrap for that because I'm done being quiet. I'm done waiting. You let him know Wozi stopped by."

The girl waltzed out and Morgan slammed the door. She was filled with so much rage that it blinded her. She flipped the lock and dropped the gun as she pressed two hands into the door and bowed her head in grief. A change had come, and Morgan knew that they wouldn't survive.

CHAPTER 4

Yo, my G. No daredevil shit tonight. You give that bitch plenty of room to come to a stop," Meek warned, as he straddled his Yamaha and stared Isa down with stern eyes.

"I need the thrill, boy. I got my part covered, you just worry about busting that bitch open," Isa stated.

The pair put the ski masks over their faces and then put helmets on top of those, leather gloves on their hands, leather jackets on their frame, all black everything.

"Aye, lover boy, where your head at?" Isa asked, turning his attention to Messiah.

"On this money, where it's always at, bitch-ass nigga," Messiah cracked. Messiah looked at the phone screen. He had sent Morgan a text. His normal routine. An emoji of a butterfly. Their form of 'I love you' but she hadn't responded. She always responded. His gut churned.

He slid his phone in his pocket and started his bike. He gripped the throttle and the brake, simultaneously, making his engine come alive, as his tires spun, burning rubber.

"Eyes up," Meek called, a ritual, the thing he said before every job, to let the team know to stay on point. The trio took off.

The highway was deserted at this hour. They passed a few straggling cars on their way North, but they knew the two-lane highway the semi they had targeted would be empty. It took them an hour to ride up on the driver. It was all fun and games, as the trio raced and hit wheelies, doing tricks, blowing time, until they saw the taillights ahead. They were connected by the Bluetooths in their helmets.

"We got action," Isa said, his voice floating through Messiah's helmet. He was right on schedule. Messiah pressed play on his handles and Kendrick Lamar filled his ears.

This what gods feel like.
Yeah, laughing to the bank like ahaa.

He hit the throttle and the machine beneath him lunged forward. Isa sped past them both, passing the truck. He always led, Messiah took the middle, handling the driver, and Meek blew the doors off the back. Team work made the dream work.

Isa sped in front of the truck, and without warning, he turned his bike into the path of the semi.

"Nigga, give yourself room," Messiah shouted into the Bluetooth. Isa was a daredevil and he gave minimum leeway for the 40-ton truck to come to a complete stop. It took a semi much longer to slow its speed, without fishtailing. Isa was only a few hundred feet in front of the truck. They had the stopping distance down to a science, but Messiah liked to leave room for error. If the driver was sleepy, or not paying attention and his reaction time was off by even a few seconds, Isa would be a memory.

Messiah's chest tightened, as he watched the brake lights illuminate on the truck. Then, he heard the horn.

HONKKKK!

"I got it," Isa replied, cockily.

The truck fishtailed, slightly, as the driver panicked, realizing that Isa wasn't moving out of its path.

Messiah reduced his speed, lining up with the door of the truck and pulling his gun, aiming it at the windshield. He pulled the trigger twice. Warning shots, to let the driver know he'd blow a hole through something if he didn't pull over. The driver skirted to a stop, pulling over onto the shoulder of the highway, right on point where they had a U-Haul tucked away, hidden in the brush on the side. The semi stopped a yard in front of Isa, who had two guns pointed at the front of the windshield.

Meek slid to a stop, turning his bike sideways and hopping off. Messiah pulled off and opened the driver's door.

"Please, man, I don't want no trouble," the driver said, with his hands up. Messiah pulled him from the truck, sending him flying to the concrete, and then sent a bullet through the radio. He heard the shotgun, as Meek popped the lock off the back and Messiah walked the driver to the rear.

"Get your ass in there," Messiah coached. "We got three minutes," Messiah called out. They cleared as much as they could from the semi in that time, and then drove their bikes into the back of the U-Haul. Messiah grabbed the driver.

"Where's your cell phone?" he barked.

The man dug in his pockets, with shaky hands, and Messiah snatched the phone, tossing it to the side of the road, before locking the man in the back of the truck. They hopped into the U-Haul and pulled away into the night. Easy money.

It took all night for the crew to inventory the take.

"This good money, G," Meek said.

"We'll put it out in the streets, Saturday. I'll be busy tomorrow," Messiah said.

"Mo got that ass locked down," Isa cracked.

"I'm taking that trip upstate," Messiah said.

Isa and Meek steeled, as they both looked at him in shock. Messiah pulled the door to their storage locker closed and put the lock on before turning to his crew.

"That mean one of two things. We either going through with the play or we pulling it off the table," Meek said. "And since Morgan clearly complicates things…"

"It's off," Messiah confirmed.

"Yo, Unc gon' spazz," Isa said.

"I'll handle him," Messiah said. "I ain't even stopping by the crib first. I'm headed that way now. It can't wait."

Meek nodded. "We on the ready either way, bruh," he said. "Just let us know the word, when you find out."

Isa's phone rang, and he pulled it from his pocket, smirking.

"Let me guess…Ali?" Messiah said.

Isa tucked his phone and then hopped on his bike. "Nah…"

"Yeah, okay," Messiah snickered. "I know what that college thang do to a nigga, bro. Shit's like quicksand. Don't get stuck."

Isa shook his head but couldn't contain the smirk that played on his lips. He held up two fingers to the side of his tattooed forehead, saluting his goodbye, before he took off.

Meek departed next. "Get at me when you get back, bro."

"Yup," Messiah called out, before riding out in the opposite direction. He was headed to face the one man who terrified him...the only man who terrified him...his father.

Messiah sat across from Reggie "Bookie" Grant. The tension at the table could be cut with a knife. Messiah took in his father's features and it was like staring into a magic ball, looking at himself, years aged.

"You want to tell me about Morgan Atkins?" Bookie asked.

"We not talking about her," Messiah said.

Bookie chuckled, as he closed the novel that was in his hand. "You dictating a lot these days. One shot of good pussy got you thinking you the boss?" Bookie asked. "Huh?"

"I dictate that. I'll kill a nigga over that," Messiah stated. "Any boy can lay down over that. I'll pop a mu'fucka just to get behind these walls and take care of a nigga that say her name the wrong way in this bitch. Even you, old man, now play with me."

The threat was clear. Messiah hadn't come to pussyfoot. This wasn't a friendly father/son visit. He was there to place his flag in the sand. He had straddled the line between the Williams clan and the Okafors, he'd finally pledged allegiance. He was rocking with Ethic. Morgan was on that side. It was the only side that mattered. Wherever she was, it was where Messiah would be. He didn't care who he had to snake to get to her.

He saw lightning strike in his father's eyes and Bookie leaned into the table, sneering. His gaze deadpanned right on Messiah.

"So, you aligning yourself with the man that killed your brother? The family that put me behind these walls? That's what you telling me? Benny Atkins set me up and put me behind these bars for the rest of my life."

"Blood ain't always family. Sometimes, family is the people who choose you," Messiah said.

"I will send a nigga to slit that pretty piece of pussy in half, fuck her real good before they cut her throat. Maybe that'll get you focused," Bookie sneered. Messiah was over the table before he could stop himself.

Messiah banged Bookie's head against the concrete so hard that blood leaked from Bookie's ear.

He was pulled off his father by armed guards and placed in cuffs, immediately. "I will fucking kill you. Erase you, nigga! I ain't the same weak-ass little boy you used to lock in closets. Be careful with me, BOOKIE." Messiah was rabid, as he spit on his father, in a blind rage, as he bucked against the guards who apprehended him.

"You just made your bed, son!" Bookie shouted, as he struggled to his feet, snatching away from the guard that tried to assist him.

Nah, you just dug your grave, pussy, Messiah thought, as they dragged him out of the visitation room.

CHAPTER 5

The panic that filled Alani when she opened her eyes crippled her. There was so much indecision, so much guilt that she was managing inside her that it made her want to flee. To be a mother and make this decision. To trample all over the memory of her daughter by being with Ethic was difficult. It eroded her morality and deducted so much of her maternal instincts that she felt foolish. It was something she would fight every day she chose to stay with him. She hadn't realized how strong the urge to run would be first thing in the morning. It was when her dreams merged with her reality. Kenzie lived in one place, Ethic lived in the other. When they met, first thing, with the rising of the sun, it was like an injury. Like a bullet. Similar to the one she had plugged Ethic with. She rolled over and put burdened eyes on Ethic, sleeping beside her. He took her breath away. He was beautiful. The type of man that he was, handsome just didn't suffice. The structure of his face, even though the scars from burns long healed, was magnificent. The depth of his shade of noire was custom, like God had been forced to mix two colors to create this particular pigment. The way his chest moved up and down, as he breathed slowly, the definitive lines that separated the muscles he worked hard to keep lean but strong. His wide nose, full beard, pillowed lips. She inched over to him, invading his space. He had a peculiar scent to him, cologne, mixed with her sex and it was lovely. It was their chemistry; the aftermath of their lovemaking and he wore it well. She would douse him in it every night, just so she could wake up to it in the morning. She had missed him terribly. She was back now, fighting turmoil, but it was worth the battle. Eight hours' worth of trapped air blew from his nose, and it came along with a light snore and she smiled. Even his morning breath was perfect. They had missed so many milestones in their relationship. There was no dating, there was no getting to know one another's favorite colors, no simplicity, just straight to complicated. Straight to fighting and fucking. Alani didn't want to skip those little steps. If the difficult things were the foundation of a house, the simple things were the paint on the walls, and everyone wanted the perfect aesthetic. She nuzzled beneath him, infiltrating his space. He laid on his side, with one hand tucked behind his ear, and she used that bicep as her pillow, then wrapped one arm around his waist. His dick pressed into her, hard and strong. Temptation. A reminder that she would die if she ever had to imagine him with another. Green eyes popped into her mind and she pinched her forehead. Damn, just the thought injured her so greatly. She opened his legs with one thigh, scooting closer and he groaned, but opened to her.

"I've got to leave before the kids wake up," she whispered. That one sentence put a gloom over the room. It was the exact way their day had started the morning she had found out about his role in her daughter's death…almost the same words. Alani felt a stir in her soul.

"Damn if you do," Ethic replied, voice gruff, like it was hitting potholes on the way out of his dry throat. It was a duet of baritone and sleepiness. He was fighting the haze, trying to awaken for her, and it was a lovely melody. He hadn't even opened his eyes yet, but he spoke. "They know you. They love you, baby. Ain't no more of that. The hiding. The fighting it. They can see you."

"But what if something changes? I just want to be sure…"

His lids lifted, and dark storms spun in his irises. Worry. Fear of losing her, again, lived there.

"Nothing's changing. Whatever I got to do to keep you here, I'm going to do," Ethic said.

Alani closed the space between his face and hers, kissing him. Neither cared about the staleness in the air between them. He inhaled her, using his strength to roll her onto her back, as he filled her all in one motion. He parted her essence without asking and she acquiesced, blooming around him. He never released her lips and Alani smiled. To have this type of love to wake to, to call her own, without pretenses, made her feel lucky. Sex at night, sex in the morning, sex whenever she wanted because he was hers. She had to stop punishing herself for that and just relish in it. This feeling, this mental orgasm that accompanied his love making was unlike anything she had ever experienced. His mouth left hers and a moan escaped her. His victim. He moved to her neck and then pulled back to wrap those full lips around her areola, swirling his tongue around the dark circle, pulling on her taut nipple, making her body scream.

How he could focus on pleasing her in so many places, Alani didn't know. Alani couldn't walk and chew gum at the same time without fucking up and biting her tongue. The rhythm of his strokes deepened, as he wrapped one arm beneath her body and pulled her into him, while still paying the utmost attention to her breasts. This nigga was an assassin and he was murdering her pussy. Missionary had never felt like such a thrill. He worked her over too thoroughly to call it bland. It was perfect. It allowed her to see him, and for him to see her, for their connection to be witnessed. It was intimate, and it was her favorite way to partake in him, on top of her, warming her, securing her, as his dick entered her and worked its way right up her stomach and tapped on her heart. Alani's legs trembled, and he lifted slightly, gripping her calves, raising them in the air, pushing them backward, so he could go deeper. Her knees met her ears, and Alani normally would have tensed, but with Ethic, Alani trusted him. She lost it in bed with him. The cautions she used with every man before him, disappeared. He was such a grown man. He never rushed. He never hurt her by chasing his own pleasure. He escorted her toward hers. Leading, guiding them both to a place so sweet that Alani felt hypnotized. It was the little things he did, like the kiss to her left calf that made her delirious. He left no part of her unloved. What man saw the value in a calf? Ethic. Only him. He needed to teach a class on how to make a woman feel appreciated. So many men around the world could learn a thing or three. Women would go to the ends of the earth for a man like Ezra Okafor. There would be no fighting, no power struggle, no back talk. If every man was a model of this man, women would submit willingly. The level of security he provided allowed room for a woman's vulnerability. No need to be hard, when a man kept you this safe and allowed you to be soft. No need to lead when he never got lost...never led you astray. No need to control when he had everything under his control. No room for worry because he expressed none; and if he did, she didn't know it. No need to question because he didn't fill her with insecurity and then call her crazy for expressing doubt. No stress. No inadequacy. God. Ethic was luxury and he was providing her with a standard. Excellence was becoming her expectation, and nothing less would suffice. If Alani ever left him again, she would have to prepare herself for loneliness because no one could ever replace him.

"Stop fighting it, baby. I feel you. Give me that shit," he groaned, lowering into her ear and then biting the lobe softly.

"Agh!" Alani cried out, as she erupted.

"Just like that," he coached.

Spasms hit her, and she shook beneath him.

"Damn," he groaned.

He put both hands on her waist, pulling her onto him, as he picked up his pace. He was close. The tension on his face gave him away. He rolled back on his thighs, lifting her body onto him as he came. Hours of lovemaking weren't necessary with Ethic, although she often received them, but he was a master with a hot 20 minutes. It was like he was a chef whipping up a quick meal, making dinner of her body, using each second wisely so it wouldn't take all day. Even when it was a quick meal, it was always excellent.

"Ohh… shit," he moaned. She clung to him, sweat acting as glue to their skin. Her breasts against his chest, her lips on his, his tongue meeting hers. Mind-blowing.

"My kids can see you," he reiterated.

It was how he got his way. He fucked her into submission. He didn't play fair, but Alani offered no protest.

She nodded, as she nuzzled her nose with his, staring him in the eyes, in a trance. So, in love. She sighed, leaving her dream behind. She could do this. She could split her day right down the middle, being loyal to her child in her sleep and loving Ethic all the hours that she was awake. She knew her nights would grow shorter. Now that she had a game plan, now that she had set some rules. She would want to spend less hours asleep and more awake, encompassed in this love.

"I can't stay," she whispered.

She felt him tense. "Nannie's home," she explained, quickly, not wanting him to get the wrong idea. "She'll need my help this morning with breakfast and bathing and things like that. She can do it herself, but with the stroke and everything, I just need to make sure I'm there."

He nodded.

"Or she can be here. You can be here. I can hire help." he whispered. "Move in with me."

Alani ran her fingers up the back of his neck, rubbing, massaging, still in his lap because he wouldn't let her go.

"I don't want to skip steps, Ethic. We missed so many things," Alani whispered.

"You want to slow down?" Ethic asked, face reflecting displeasure.

"I want to..." she paused and then shrugged. "I don't know...date you," she said. "I want to wait by the front door in a pretty dress and feel butterflies while I wait for you to show up. I want to fill in all those holes. I want easy memories with you, not just these grand moments of intensity. I want you to take me on a trip one day. I want to kiss you goodnight and then call you on the way home because I miss you as soon as you drive off. I want to hold your hand on Sundays in church. I want to rebuild our history," she fantasized. He knew she had thought of these things before because of the whimsical way in which she expressed them.

"Date you, huh?" he said. He laid her on her back and kissed her lips, a quick peck, and then climbed out of bed.

"Is that okay?" she asked.

He ran his hand down his beard and then scratched the back of his head, as his brows rose.

"Yeah, that's okay," he said. He wanted more. She knew it, but this process was important. Alani came up on her knees, beaming, as she hobbled to the edge of the mattress where he stood.

She looked up at him. "Thank you," she said.

She climbed out of bed and headed to the shower. When she got to the doorway, she turned and saw him sitting on the side of his bed, head in his hands. Such an intense man. Yes, dating would lighten him some. It would be lighthearted.

They would experience fun together. They needed that. She imagined he hadn't partaken in fun in a very long time. "Shower sex is a part of dating, sir."

He smirked, as his gaze lifted.

She curled her finger, beckoning him, before walking backwards into the bathroom, disappearing from his sights.

Alani stepped into his shower and relished under the stream of hot water. It only took seconds for Ethic to join her. She felt the cool air infiltrate her space, as he climbed in, then the hair on his strong thighs, as he nestled against her behind. He hardened, and she moaned, as he reached around her body, grabbing her breasts, tweaking her nipples with expertise. He sat on the built-in tiled seat and pulled her down onto him. His lips kissed her back, as she rode him. His hand on her hips, guiding her rhythm, because he was so damn filling that Alani had to go slow at first to get used to the magnificence of it all. Alani had never had a man make her want sex so much. She could count on one hand how many times she had opened her legs because she wanted to indulge in it with other men. With Ethic, every time, she was game…every time, she craved it…she never tired of it…never sickened of any of it…his touch, his stroke, the taste of him. He was so skilled at pleasing her. So unselfish. He wrapped one arm around her body and gripped her neck, as he forced her back against his chest, while rising to match her with deep strokes. Her mouth fell open, as the shower rained over them, steam rising around them, thickening the air.

His other hand found her clit and rolled it like he was shaping small beads of Play-Doh between two fingers.

He bit her shoulder and she never knew teeth could feel so erotic. It sent shock waves to her clit and he squeezed and rolled and kneaded it and she fell into spasms as she rained her love all over him.

"Yesss," she whispered. Her head fell back against his shoulder, as she tried to catch her breath. His kisses against her neck and ear were so gentle, so appreciative. Full of adoration. He was painting her with love and adding colors to her gray world. She felt it. Every time he touched her, even more when he brought her to orgasm, the energy, the love he left in her, on her…like a stain to her soul, he was pouring something into her that she would never be able to get rid of. Alani lifted from his lap and dropped to her knees, taking him into her mouth because she wanted him to pour more. She wanted him to pour it all. To fill her with his essence because his DNA felt like nourishment. It kept her soul full. His toes curled, and he fisted her hair, as he watched and gritted his teeth.

"Ohh, shit," he groaned, as he emptied himself. Alani decided then and there that there was no point in counting her orgasms with this man. Deciding to love him was like buying an unlimited wristband at the fair. She got unlimited rides. He gripped her shoulders, pulling her to her feet, as he kissed her under the shower head.

He washed himself and then her before climbing out the shower.

Wrapped in plush towels, they entered his bedroom.

A knock at the door made Alani freeze. Her eyes widened in alarm. Busted. She felt like they had been caught red-handed with their hands inside the cookie jar. Ethic kissed her lips. "Relax," he said. "You belong here."

"Daddy, don't forget about my awards assembly at school. Eazy's is today too," Bella called through the door.

"I got you, baby girl," he said. "Alani and I will be out in a bit."

"Alani's here? Morning, Alani!"

Ethic heard the joy in his daughter's voice. He hadn't gotten a good morning. Bella had gotten straight down to business with him, but Alani, Bella beamed for. Monday morning blues had no wins against the presence of Alani in his home. He shook his head, smiling because he understood. It was the Friday-est Monday ever.

Alani felt odd calling through the door. Her belly tightened and apprehension filled it as she called out. "Good morning, B! I'll be down to cook breakfast. Give me 10 minutes."

"Lily's cooking lox and eggs…"

"I'll be down to cook you real breakfast," Alani called back.

"Thank God!" Eazy's voice was now behind the door.

"Morning, Alani!" Eazy called too.

Ethic turned to Alani, with his arms held out. "What am I? The help? I can't get no love with you here, huh?"

Her smile warmed him. He snatched her towel from her body, and then pulled her near.

She giggled. So lighthearted…so carefree and it felt wonderful. She had lived 30 years of her life without feeling this type of joy, and she had no idea how she had ever survived.

She kissed him and then maneuvered out of his embrace, because she was naked, and he was wearing only a towel and that was bound to lead to more sex. Neither of them had the time they would make to accommodate the pulse she could already feel reviving between her thighs. She began to dress.

"I completely forgot about the ceremony at B's school. I'm going to have to see if Mo can swing by the house to get her tuition payment. I was supposed to head to State to drop it off, but I can't do both," Ethic said.

"I can drop it off for you. I've got to meet the contractors today to do some work on the last few houses, and stop by the college to check in on the progress of my publishing contract; but after that, I can link with Morgan," Alani offered. "I wish I could come to the ceremony for the kids, but I've been trying to finish these houses for weeks. It's the first time I've been able to nail down a date with the contractor to meet to discuss the final details. I'll make them a special dinner tonight to make up for it."

Damn, if this didn't feel good to him. Her contributions. Her partnership. Her eagerness to help parent his children, to please him, to love them all. He looked at her in awe.

"What?" she asked.

"That God thing that you're trying to get me to believe in..."

"Yeah," she said, squinting.

"He had to make you. I believe that," Ethic said.

Alani slipped into her jeans and walked over to him. "Yeah, well, he made you too, Mr. Okafor. He's all up and through you."

Alani opened the door, and just before she was out the room, Ethic said, "I'm going to send you Messiah's address. You don't have to drive all the way to State. You can drop the check off to him later. He'll make the run for me. You just hurry home to me."

"Will do," she said, with a smile. This felt routine. This felt normal. As Alani descended the stairs and heard the voices of laughter from two children she adored, she had to admit... it felt like home; and for the first time, she carried no guilt about being a part of it.

CHAPTER 6

Morgan sat on the couch. He took her in, breath catching in his chest because she was fucking exquisite. The heather grey sports bra and panties she wore rested against her light skin. The words CALVIN KLEIN wrapped around the elastic band of her bra and the top of her panties. Even that made him jealous. Another man's name on her body. Even if it was a label. His red and black, checkered, button-down shirt was like a robe over her shoulders, warming her, slightly, as it hung lazily on one side. There wasn't a damn thing little about little Morgan anymore. She was a bad bitch, and as he eyed the pizza box beside her, he wondered if she had answered the door like this. Messiah wanted to murder something.

Morgan sat back, one leg propped up on the living room table, her back slouched against the red, leather sofa. Rockstud heeled booties rested on her feet and he knew she must have been breaking in a new pair because she walked around in heels all day like they were house shoes. "To stretch them for when I dance," she would explain. Her hair was middle-parted and bone straight. A blunt was pinched between her fingers, as she brought it to her red-painted lips. She took a hit. Something she rarely did, and she tilted her head back, as she released the smoke slowly. That shit swayed out of her mouth like an exotic dancer, seducing the air. His dick jumped.

"Sit down, Messiah," she said.

His brows lifted. She was bothered. He knew her too well not to know that much and her tone was lethal.

"What's wrong, shorty?"

Morgan hit the blunt, again. He tried to scroll through his mental Rolodex to pin point the source of her disdain. Had she found something in his crib? A condom? That would certainly put her in a mood because they never used any. A random phone number? He had nothing to hide, but he wondered if something old had come back to disrupt the peace in his relationship. From the look on her face, something was awry. Messiah wouldn't even have entertained this conversation… this clear 'G checking', a reprimand from anyone EXCEPT her. He sat in the chair and leaned forward, elbows to knees, as he looked her in the eyes.

"I feel like some bullshit is about to come out those pretty-ass lips," Messiah said, as he rubbed his hands together in anticipation. He was high. The lids of his eyes, mere slits, from the blunt he had smoked on the way home.

"Who the fuck is Wozi?" she asked.

Messiah's hands stopped moving and he stood. Morgan reached for the pizza box, pulling out the handgun he had given her. She put it in her lap, finger on the trigger.

"I said sit down," she said, but her voice skipped on the track like an old-school CD. Her eyes misted. Messiah lifted his hands.

"Mo…"

"So, while you were off doing who knows what…you got a visit, Messiah," she said.

"Mo, I can explain…"

"You can explain a bitch showing up at your house? Carrying a baby on her hip?" Morgan asked.

Messiah paused.

"The same house you told me you only bring people you trust too. People you love? Your words not mine," Mo said, as she brought the blunt to her lips and inhaled again. Fuck the baby in her stomach because she had already decided she wouldn't be baby mama #2. *Fuck I look like?* She thought, growing angrier, her temper steeping like tea, marinating, growing stronger. She blew out the smoke, as she pierced him with her eyes. "You can explain a bitch telling me to tell you that you can't hide your family?" Morgan asked. She wasn't yelling. He wished she was. She was detaching. This calm was scary. He zeroed in on the bags on the side of the couch. How hadn't he noticed them before?

Messiah swiped both hands down his face. He was stuck. Stuck between what he should say and what he couldn't?

Morgan sneered, as she flicked the lit blunt at him, making him stand to brush the hot narcotic from his shirt.

"Yo, what the fuck?!" he shouted. He moved to come around the table, but Morgan lifted the gun.

"Ah, ah," she said. Her composure was terrifying. Messiah stood, frozen like she had put up a stop sign. Red light, green light, nigga. Nobody had ever stopped him in his tracks before, but here was his queen…little Morgan, Mo Money, the pretty, little, deaf girl that he had given his heart too, commanding his every move. His palms were out at his side, at her mercy.

"All that loyalty shit you talk," she scoffed, as she shook her head. She was so angry she couldn't cry, so angry that she was biting the flesh on the inside of her cheek. She tasted blood.

"Baby, she ain't shit. I swear to God I'm not cheating on you, Mo. I promise you. I promise, baby," Messiah said. It was all he could say. It wasn't an explanation, but what she assumed was better than the truth. It was less damaging than the secret he was hiding from her.

"Oh no, you're not cheating on me. That bitch has a baby. You're cheating on her. You're just lying to me. You out here selling dreams and I'm buying them bitches in bulk. You're fucking me daily, knowing…" She paused because tears were coming, and she didn't want to cry. She pointed the gun at him. Red means dead. Safety off. Oh, the temperament of a young girl's heart. Messiah had fucked up. She was seconds off the trigger and the aggression he had taught her had her contemplating pulling it. She shook her head. "I'm off this. I'm done, Messiah."

He felt his chest tighten when she bent to reach for her bags. It felt like his entire world was crashing.

"Mo! No, shorty. No, baby, stop. Just give me a second…"

He couldn't believe it was his voice coming out of his mouth. Begging anybody to stay in his life was a foreign concept. Messiah had turned into Keith Sweat, he was pleading so hard. All he needed was a smooth beat to lace his voice and he would have a hit record. He couldn't let Morgan leave.

The doorbell rang, and Morgan started for it. Messiah was right on top of her.

"Don't fucking touch me!" she shouted, as she snatched open the door. Aria and Isa stood on the other side.

"No, baby, listen…" Messiah said. He was pleading, as she pushed out of the house.

"You shouldn't have brought him, Aria," Morgan snapped.

"What's going on?" Aria shrieked, caught off guard. "You just said to come over…you didn't say come alone! What the fuck is up?" Aria shrieked, as she eyed the gun in Morgan's hand.

"I just need a ride back to my place," Morgan said. She handed Aria a bag and then went back for the other one. Messiah trailed her like a dog.

"She don't need no fucking ride!" Messiah barked, as he snatched the bag from Morgan's hand. "She's not going no fucking where."

"Messiah…" Aria stated, looking back and forth between the couple.

"No! Bro, get her the fuck out my crib, my G, before I lose my temper," Messiah said, pointing at Isa.

Morgan aimed the gun, point blank at Messiah's head. "Lose your temper, nigga," she grit. Messiah had never seen this side to Morgan. This was all him. He had put all this gangster in her. She was him and now she was leaving. He had given her all he had to give - his identity. If she left, who would he be? "So I can lose mine."

"Please, Mo. Hear me out," he said, his eyes were glossing over. Isa stepped up.

"Speak, Messiah! You not saying nothing. Who is Wozi? I don't hear nothing. Who. The. Fuck. Is. Wozi?" Morgan jabbed his ass with every word. Then, she pointed the gun to his chest. "You broke my whole heart, Messiah. Riddled that shit without thinking twice."

Isa hit Messiah with shocked eyes and Messiah put both hands on his head, as he turned his back to Morgan.

"Mo. Sis. Put the gun down," Isa said.

"Keep him away from me, while I get the rest of my stuff, before I shoot his cheating-ass," she said, finally breaking, lip trembling as tears fell. "Dirty-dick-ass nigga," she mumbled, while shaking her head in disappointment. She let the gun hang on her finger, letting go of the handle in surrender. Isa took it. Messiah sat where he stood, right there on the floor, elbows to knees, head hanging in despair, as Morgan headed for the bedroom.

Aria inched by him. "I'm going to go try to calm her down," she said. "Keep him in here." Isa nodded.

"Don't let her leave me," Messiah whispered. Aria heard so much hurt in his voice that her eyes misted. She nodded and then rushed after Morgan.

Isa rubbed his waves. "Wozi?"

"I'm slapping fire from her stupid-ass," Messiah said.

"Paint the picture for me, bro. So, Mo knows?" Isa asked.

Messiah shook his head. "Nah, she don't know that. Wozi on some bullshit. Mo thinks she's a chick I'm busting

70

down. She came over here with the baby on her hip, talking some bullshit. Got it looking like I'm cheating..."

"Ain't that better than the alternative?" Isa countered. "Let her breathe for a few days and get Wozi in check. It's only so long you gon' be able to balance this shit, bro. We either got to move on the shit or put the shit to bed. You lose her either way."

"You think I don't know that?" Messiah asked. The question erupted out of him, in frustration. He stood to his feet, as Morgan and Aria came down the staircase.

She was fully dressed and carried the rest of her belongings in his duffel bag. Her face was red, and it ate away at him because he knew she had gone upstairs to cry.

"If you leave me, I'm a dead man, Mo. The shit's going to kill me, shorty, because I'm gon' go full force into this shit. Without you, I'm going to jail or I'm dying out here, Mo."

Morgan stopped at the door. She closed her eyes, as tears welled in her eyes. The thought of either filled her with a hole so massive that she could fall inside it herself.

Messiah stood and approached Morgan, wrapping a hand around her waist to pull her into him. He put his lips on the back of her neck and kissed there.

"I'm not cheating on you. Another bitch is the last thing on my mind. You have to trust that what you feel, how I make you feel, is real," he mumbled. Morgan closed her eyes. The sound of gravel crunching, as a car pulled curbside, popped them back open.

"Bro..." Isa said. Messiah looked up and Morgan pulled

away, as the woman who had stirred up all the trouble emerged from the car.

"You almost had me," Morgan scoffed. "She's pulling up to your house like it's her shit. Like I'm sleeping in her bed. Clearly, I'm in the way. Let me remove myself." Morgan snatched out of his grasp and began crumbling, as soon as she took the first step. Morgan's chin quivered, as she tried to escape. The girl stood against her car, arms folded across her chest, face pulled tight in perturb. Morgan wanted to hate her, but this was Messiah's doing.

"Mo…" Messiah came after her, closing Aria's car door, before she could climb inside.

"Who is she, Messiah?"

"Messiah, cancel this shit and send the bitch on her way. Now," Wozi piped up.

Morgan's neck whipped in Wozi's direction. She chuckled. "Cancel me? I was trying to not be that chick that blamed the other woman for a nigga's lies, but don't try me."

Messiah turned to Wozi, pointing a stern finger. "Yo, Wozi. Shut the fuck up! Get in the car and wait!" He turned to Morgan, gripping her waist, holding her back.

"Mo…"

She couldn't believe she was standing here, arguing with another woman over Messiah. Her Messiah. He was hers. How was he even allowing this to occur?

"Better get this bitch, Messiah, before I tell her some shit that'll hurt her little feelings," the girl said.

Morgan's eyes widened, her stomach plummeted, and her heart sank. She pulled away from Messiah, pointing her stiletto-shaped fingernails in the shape of a gun in the direction of this girl. She felt a shift in the atmosphere and she knew that today was the last day that she would be happy for a very long time. If she had known, she would have relished in it a little more, but life didn't work that way. Things were right until they were wrong, and by then, it was too late to appreciate the little things that had been insignificant before sadness became important. Like the forehead kisses he gave her. Something small felt huge now because she had a feeling she wouldn't be receiving anymore from now on.

"I'll slap the shit out of you, ho! Who you think you talking to? Hurt my feelings?" Morgan was so livid that she swung on Messiah. "Stop touching me, nigga! You're protecting her? Who is this bitch? Whose feelings is she hurting?"

Morgan was like a category five storm, as she tried to get around Messiah. He put his hand to her chest. "Mo, chill."

"Yeah, Morgan Atkins, sister of Raven Atkins, daughter of Benny Atkins, chill!"

Messiah had Morgan hemmed up, as she dipped, twisted, and turned, trying her hardest to bulldoze through him. Hearing the names of her dead family members was like gasoline to fire. Who was this girl? She seemed to know everything about Morgan, yet Morgan knew nothing about her. Messiah was winded, as he grappled with her, trying his best to keep her contained without harming her. He picked her up by the waist and then turned to the girl behind him with fire in his eyes. "Shut the fuck up and get in the car!"

"She better before she get done up out here," Aria threatened, as she watched the scene unfold.

"Yo, baby girl, this ain't your beef," Isa said, putting a leash on Aria.

"Nigga, who are you, my daddy? I pop off when I want to pop off, and right now, I'm feeling real froggy," Aria stated, challenging Wozi. "We ain't even fucking yet. Boy, bye."

Isa smirked, trapping her, as he wedged her between the car and his body, looking down at her while licking his lips. "Yet, huh?"

Wozi held up her hands and shook her head in surrender. "You niggas and these young-ass girls. Handle that bitch, Messiah, and let's go," she snapped. Aria was like a dog out a race gate. She ran across the lawn, but Isa intercepted her, picking her up by the waist and pinning her against the car. Aria tied her long hair up, as Isa held her firmly in place.

"That's okay, bitch. He can't hold me back forever," Aria said, nodding her head. She was already on 'go'.

Everyone was yelling. Aria. Morgan. Wozi waved them off, unbothered.

"Handle me? Go? He ain't going nowhere with your dusty-ass. This me! Every inch of this nigga is mine! You bum!" She was so out of character, she didn't recognize herself. All she saw was red, all she heard was yelling, all she felt was anguish. Messiah couldn't stop her, so he picked her up and carried her over his shoulder into the house.

Anger pulsed through her and she attacked him, instantly. "Who is she, Messiah?" He could practically see the steam coming from her ears.

He grabbed her hands and pinned them above her head, trapping her body against the door with his. Guilt lived in his eyes. She didn't need his words. His body language spoke volumes. Sickness overcame Morgan.

"Noooo," she cried, as she hit the back of her head against the door, again and again, trying to wake herself up because this had to be a bad dream. Her eyes pleaded with him, as they watered. His heart cracked in his chest. He had known this day would come. When the truth destroyed everything he had built with her. "Siah…no, no. How could you do this to us?" Morgan was melting, legs turning to goo beneath her, as she slid down the door in despair. "This is me…You said I was yours."

Messiah kneeled with her, trying to scoop her into his arms, trying to build her back up, put her pieces back together but she was destroyed. It was like seeing Wozi and Messiah in the same space had made her inconsolable.

"Mo," he whispered. "Shorty…" He had no explanations to give. He could break her heart with the lie or break it with the truth.

She sat with her elbows on her knees, head lifted to the sky, face drenched from her tears. Agony spread her lips wide, as she tried her hardest to hold in these cries. Messiah moved the hair from her face, reminding her what his touch felt like, how gentle she made him. The thought of his hands touching the girl outside flashed through her mind in a split second and she swatted his hands away. Her nostrils flared, and she buried her hands in her hair, pulling at the roots, as if she was trying to snatch the image from her brain. She was on her feet next, running out the door before Messiah could hold her back.

"Mo!" She heard him bark her name, but her feet were already flying across the pavement, toward the black Benz. She wondered if he had bought it for the girl and that pissed her off more.

Morgan's little nimble-ass turned into a world class boxer, as the girl stepped off the car with her hands raised. The momentum from Morgan running full speed, plus the punch she threw, sent the girl over the side of the convertible. Morgan had zero fucks to give. She never let up. With a hand full of hair balled in her fist, Morgan threw blow after blow. She had the girl stuffed in the bottom of the backseat, head first, feet up, as she leaned over the car, relentless in her attack. "Bitch!" Morgan snapped, as she tagged the girl. She was giving an old-school ass whooping...commentating that shit like she was somebody's mama. "I." PUNCH. "TOLD." PUNCH. "YOU." PUNCH. "Not to play with me." SLAP. "HO!"

"Mo!" Messiah shouted, as he grabbed her by the waist and bear hugged her, trapping her arms.

"Ha!" Morgan shouted, as she stuck out her entire tongue, while trying to lunge over Messiah's shoulders. "Bitch! Who the fuck you think I am? Don't run up on me on some woman to woman shit. Over this nigga, here? I'ma beat your ass every time I see you! Play with me!"

Wozi attacked and with Messiah's attention on Morgan, he didn't realize he was putting her at a disadvantage until he felt the fist fly over his shoulder for Morgan. Aria slipped loose from Isa and broke across the lawn.

WHOP! WHOP!

Wozi took two to the back of the head from the sneak from Aria, before Isa could rein her in.

"We don't fight fair, bitch! She swing! I'm swinging!" Aria shouted over Isa's shoulder.

"Period!" Morgan shouted. Wozi was still trying to get to Morgan, throwing all types of blows over Messiah, as Messiah bear hugged Morgan, protecting her, as her little-ass tried to shake him loose. It was chaos. Messiah turned and the malice in his stare stopped Wozi mid-swing. This was bad. It was loud and out of hand. So much was at jeopardy. How had he let this catch up to him? "GO TO THE FUCKING CAR!" he barked.

"Yeah, bitch, skedaddle," Morgan goaded. Her mouth was reckless, when provoked, but with Messiah as the muse shaping her attitude, her bite was vicious too. "I was gon' give him back to you, bitch. Now, I just might keep his dog-ass! Put him on a leash and make him lick something for a treat, bitch."

Yes, Morgan was talking real reckless and if Messiah hadn't been so worried about losing her, he might have found the shit sexy, but he was desperate…he was terrified of what would happen next. One thing he knew for certain, Wozi stayed strapped. This could go left, if he didn't get it under control.

Messiah heaved, as he gripped the sides of Morgan's face. She pushed him. She hadn't forgotten that he was the cause of this. He was the reason she was coming out of character, tagging bitches in the middle of the street. The part that pissed her off most was that she had never seen the betrayal coming. He was so good at pretending…he put up such a good act of loyalty. She felt stupid. Her heart was broken. The anger hadn't erased the emptiness she felt.

"You said I was different," she sobbed. "You promised to be different for me!" He pressed his forehead to hers and closed his eyes at the feeling of her wet tears, as he kissed her lips.

"You are, Mo. I just fucked up, shorty. I'm fucked up," he said, his voice cracking. "I swear to God I love you. I love you, shorty. It's some shit I got to clean up but that's gon' always be a true story."

She pulled her hands from his grasp and jabbed him, and then slapped him. Messiah's type of crazy absorbed the blows. He liked the rage, the pain, but if he didn't stop her, she was going to do real damage. He hemmed her up, catching her wrists with one hand and pulling her into him with the other. "Stop, shorty. Stop…" he whispered, in her ear. He was pleading. Her breakdown was devastating to witness. She was touching him, on the inside, her disappointment searing him. His insides had never felt this tender.

"Morgan?"

Morgan turned, stunned, to find Alani standing on the porch. Suddenly, all the ill feelings Morgan had toward her, all the jealousy and animosity… it all just dissipated. In that moment, Morgan needed her. She rushed to Alani, sobs spilling from her, devastation overflowing. Alani wrapped Morgan in her arms, as she looked at Messiah in confusion. Her eyes darted around the scene, as she tried to piece together the story without verbalizing questions.

She knew whatever had occurred it had devastated Morgan.

"Mo…"

Alani looked up in stun at the vulnerability she heard in just the way Messiah said her name. Alani put the pieces of the puzzle together. Ethic's soldier and his daughter. Forbidden love. It always led to heartbreak.

She shook her head, as Morgan melted into her. "Messiah, now might not be the best time," Alani whispered. She placed one hand around Morgan's shoulder and opened a palm under her chin. "Shhh," she consoled. Morgan was so incredibly hurt. It felt like someone was digging a hole through her. "Un uh," Alani whispered. "Hold your head up, baby girl. Don't let them see you like this."

Messiah placed the palms of his hands on top of his head, as he turned in frustration. It was so hard for him to see her this way. This was worse than the night at the hotel, when she had been raped. How had he caused her the same dismay? He had raped her heart. He felt her energy leaving him. He felt himself losing her. It was like water slipping through his fingers. He couldn't hold onto it, no matter how hard he tried. "Mo, baby…" He paused, as he chose his words carefully. "It's a lot I want to say to you, but I have somewhere I need to be…"

Morgan released Alani and wiped her tears, only for more to slide down her face. "Figure that? Somewhere you need to be," she whispered. She scoffed, in disbelief. "As if you don't need to be here? Like your obligation to me doesn't even matter." She thought of the baby growing in her stomach. She

hadn't even told him yet and he was already leaving her...
leaving them. They were already becoming those people she
feared...the ones who loved the kid but hated each other.
"*I* need you, Messiah." Her hands said those words because
she didn't want anyone else to know she was begging. "If
you leave here with her, I'll never forgive you. I'll get rid of
everything you ever wanted with me. No love. No family. It'll
be done."

He rubbed his hands over his face. He felt cornered and
Messiah only reacted one way when he felt trapped. His
entire past played in his mind. Things had been so clear
until she had come into his world to blur his vision. Now, he
loved her. Now, he was hurting her. His truth would shatter
her. The truth. He was Mizan's brother and the girl outside
wasn't some random girl he had been unfaithful with, she
was Mizan's sister, and they had been grooming Messiah for
years for revenge. She hadn't been a part of the plan. She had
deterred him from the plan. He couldn't speak that truth.
That truth would annihilate her.

"Shorty..."

"Are you leaving here with her, Messiah? Yes or no?" Her
voice trembled because she already knew the answer and
Messiah's hesitance only fueled the betrayal she felt.

Morgan shook her head, disappointment fell from her eyes,
sliding down her face, as the confidence he had filled her with
the past few months left her. "You just killed everything. I'm
done with you," she said. Alani wrapped her arms around Mo
and Morgan rested her head on Alani's shoulder, bawling,
as she walked out. Messiah watched in dismay as his reason
for breathing was put into the passenger seat of a little Prius

and driven away. He saw red. Blind fury fueled him, as he stormed out the door.

Isa was smart to tuck Aria into her car and send her away because Messiah was on a warpath and headed straight for Wozi. Isa took quick strides to intercept, but Messiah got there first.

"WHAT THE FUCK IS WRONG WITH YOU?" Messiah asked, as he wrapped his hands around his sister's neck and lifted her clean out her shoes, before slamming her hard against the hood of her car. She clawed at his hands and swung with all her might, but Messiah wouldn't let up. She had cost him everything. He could squeeze the life out of her. He could see the life leaving her, as he choked her, damn near breaking her neck from the pressure of his hold.

"Messiah! Chill!" Isa shouted. He pulled Messiah away.

Wozi scrambled, adjusting her clothes, and pulling the bloodied lip Morgan had given her into her mouth. She pointed a stern finger in his face. "Don't blame this on me! Nobody told you to start fucking Morgan Atkins! You were here for one reason! To get Ethic's connect and leave him slumped, the same way he left our brother slumped! That was it. Daddy laid out the plan clear as day and you fucking shit up!"

"I can't get to the connect! Ain't no connect! Ethic ain't in the streets no more! I've been around the nigga for years! You know what he schooling me on? Stocks! Bonds! Black history and shit! The nigga ain't even in the game. He practically raised me. He came around the block, buying a nigga new shoes because he heard the other kids teasing me about the ones I dug out the lost and found at school. He bought me new backpacks for school. He taught me how to throw a football, gave me my first rubber. I knew him before Mizan ever had a problem with him, and y'all just want me to put a bullet in his back! He was a good nigga then and he a good nigga now, and I'm underneath him, watching him, lurking like a fucking snake, waiting to bite. He got three fucking kids who need him. I've been to birthday parties and recitals and shit…"

"Fuck him! Fuck them! Mizan raised you!" Wozi defended, with tears in her eyes.

"Nah! He raised you! He was different with me! It's more to family than blood!" Messiah was so livid he spit when he spoke and jabbed a finger into her forehead. "That nigga…" Grief choked him, as his words caught in his throat. He was about to reveal too much, about to share secrets that he had promised to take to his grave. Secrets that had turned him into an aggressive little boy, an even more aggressive grown man. A man. Those secrets had made him a man because he had vowed to be so tough that nobody would ever be able to make him feel like he wasn't a man ever again.

"That nigga what? Mizan came around and made sure you had food in your stomach after Daddy went to prison. We ain't have the same mama. He didn't have to do that. He never treated us like half anything. He loved us with his whole heart. Mizan was all we had, and Ethic murdered him. That spoiled bitch you knocking down…her father set Daddy up to go to prison. Why do you think Mizan set Benny Atkins up to be arrested instead of killing him? It was payback! Why do you think he got with Raven Atkins in the first place? Payback! You the only one going against the family! Finish your plate! Daddy taught you better. You don't leave nothing on the plate. You either knock off Ethic, or I'm knocking off the bitch that got you so distracted. Your choice," Wozi said.

Messiah backed her up against the car and grit his teeth so hard his jaw hurt. He was seething, nostrils flaring, as he pointed a finger in her face. "Hear me clear, Wozi. You touch her and I'ma murk you."

"You gon' kill me, Messiah? I'm your sister. Your flesh and blood! I'm all the family you got. You ain't gon' do shit," Wozi said, pushing him away from her, hard. Two siblings, under loved, with so much aggression. They had a lot to be angry about, and what once had been a team, was now two different people with dissenting agendas. She had no idea the things Messiah had done and would do on Morgan's behalf. Wozi was wading in dangerous waters. She didn't want to put Messiah in a position to choose, because she wouldn't win. "Cut her off and get your head back in the game. Ethic or Morgan Atkins." She set out the ultimatum, as if it were a simple choice. She was on the outside, she wasn't up close to the dirt, so she could never understand how hard it would be for him to choose between them. Wozi snatched her door open and got in the car, peeling off into the night.

CHAPTER 7

E thic doesn't know." Morgan's words were solemn. She muttered them with uncertainty and a bit of fear because she knew that there was no hiding her disobedience now.

Alani took a deep breath, as she kept her eyes on the road. The last secret she had kept from Ethic had crippled them. They were just starting over. She couldn't hide this from him. She wanted to be Morgan's confidante. She wanted to melt the ice walls that hindered them from getting to know one another, but not at the expense of her relationship with Ethic. She wouldn't risk that. She couldn't afford any missteps with him. The same way he was proving his worth, she was proving hers too, making up for past mistakes. She had to be careful with the way she handled this. Asking Bella to lie for her had been strike one. Keeping Love from him was strike two. Holding a damaging secret about another one of his children would strike her out. She couldn't. This was a part of merging their lives...her finding her place with each one of his offspring...Morgan would be the hardest, but she couldn't not parent her in this moment. She couldn't try to be her friend at the sacrifice of her connection to her man. She wanted Morgan to like her. She needed her acceptance, in fact, but she wouldn't lie to get it.

"Morgan, please don't ask me to keep this from him," Alani whispered.

Morgan pierced her with wet eyes. "He's going to be so angry with me," she whispered. Alani saw nothing more than a little girl that was afraid to disappoint the most important man in her life. Ethic had done a beautiful job with his children...with Morgan. They respected him greatly, admired him, and the idea of letting him down terrified them. Alani had seen it before with Bella and now with Morgan. That wasn't a coincidence, that was consistency...every day love from a father who had never failed them. He had made good on things he had promised them over the years. It made Morgan feel guilty for not reciprocating. Ethic had fathered this girl well and it made Alani love him a little more.

"Ethic's anger is rooted in love, Morgan. His anger doesn't erase the love. It is the love. It's him wanting to stop you from making mistakes he can see coming from a mile away. I shouldn't be the one to tell him this. He should hear this from you." Morgan's chin hit her chest, as she cried. Alani reached over and rubbed Morgan's head, lovingly. She remembered the feeling of young heartbreak. Oh, how it felt like the end of the world. Those first experiences of putting your heart in the hands of some knuckleheaded-ass boy who would undoubtedly drop it. It ached like no other because young girls didn't possess the ability to bandage the wound. They just bled out. They closed themselves in their rooms and listened to love songs until they cried it all out.

"Do you love Messiah?" Alani asked.

Morgan nodded, as she wiped the snot from her nose with the back of her hand, sniffling. "So much. We were going to tell him. We were just waiting for the right time."

"Sometimes, there is no right time," Alani said, softly.

"I thought he loved me too," Morgan said, feeling foolish, as she spun the ring on her finger around. He had always been so insistent on the possibility of hurting her. His prediction had been accurate. She was crushed.

"Did his actions say the same?" Alani questioned.

"Every single day. His actions spoke the loudest. Words. Actions. It was all a lie," Morgan whispered. She blinked and effortless emotion spilled onto her face. She shook her head, in disgrace, grimacing, as if a bout of pain had suddenly overcome her. Why did it ache so bad?

"I'm sorry, Morgan. I'm sorry that you're hurting and I'm sorry that I'm the one who witnessed it. I know I'm the last person you wanted to see."

"What were you doing there anyway?" Morgan asked. "Are you and Ethic back together?"

Alani nodded. "We're trying to figure it out. He asked me to swing by to give Messiah the tuition check for your schooling. Ethic was going to ask him to bring it to you." Alani whispered. Alani pulled the check from her visor and handed it to Morgan. "Is that how this happened? Ethic put you two in the same space one too many times?"

Morgan shook her head. "I've been in love with Messiah since I was 13 years old."

"A crush?" Alani asked.

"No, it was more than that," Morgan said, passionately. "He's always been around, and I always knew I belonged to him. Like he owns me. My heart and my body and my mind is pulled to him whenever he is in a room, ever since I was a kid. He didn't see it then. It took a lot for him to ever see it because I'm so much younger than he is, but when he felt what I felt..." Morgan paused and shook her head. "Ethic didn't have to do anything. It would have happened regardless."

Morgan looked out the window, resting her head against the glass, as Alani carried her home.

When they arrived, Morgan didn't move. She sat there, staring up at the yellow lights that shined through the windows inside.

"If it's love, it will always come back," Alani said. "The darkest dark can't dim love's light, Morgan. I saw Messiah tonight. I'm staring at you right now. I don't know either of you that well, but I know what love looks like. I saw that, through the tears and the confusion and the lies...love was in attendance tonight. Ethic isn't here right now. You'll have a couple hours to figure out what you want to say. He's your father though, Morgan. There isn't much you could say or do that he wouldn't try to understand."

Morgan nodded and then climbed out the car. Alani put her key to the door and it was an odd feeling. Having a key. Unlimited access to this home...to him. She had restricted herself from him for so long that this felt like she was breaking a rule. She turned the key and pushed the door with her shoulder, entering the beautiful foyer.

Morgan headed straight for the staircase, but she stopped halfway up.

"Thank you for getting me out of there," Morgan said, voice full of woe.

Alani nodded, and Morgan retreated to her old room.

Alani stood there for a while, feeling out of place. Being there without Ethic felt odd, intrusive, like she was trespassing. Should she stay on the first floor? Was it okay to retreat to the comfort of his bedroom? Should she make dinner? Bella and Eazy were off at extra-curricular activities, being taken care of by Lily. There was really no need for Alani to stay, but he had given her the key. He had asked her to come back. "…home to me," he had said. Oh, the complications that accompanied the simplicity of having access. *Should I even be here when he gets home? Maybe I should just go home and wait for him to call.*

Alani did what felt natural and went into the kitchen. She located Ethic's speaker and plugged her phone up to it. She pressed play and a lovely melody filled the air.

I see it clear, my heart is here
We've got each other, let's take it from there
And if I could, I'd love you a forever at a time
Oohhh ohhhh

Alani closed her eyes and let her neck sway from side to side. A couple of forevers. She would only be so lucky to have that with Ethic. She went into the refrigerator and pulled out chicken. *Can't go wrong with chicken.*

She swayed to the beautiful song, as she cooked a meal. Pouring her all into it, the lyrics and the dish, as she sang.

Me and you are built like armor
Nothing can stop us from looving on uu-uus—uss
And I'm not asking for much
Just a couple of forevers

Alani had tears in her eyes, as she moved around Ethic's home. It felt so good. So, fulfilling. To be listening to this song, making a meal for a man who loved her. It was a woman's duty to keep a man fed. Women fought that role. Hated it, even, because they were so busy fulfilling so many other roles. Roles that weren't really theirs to uphold. By the time they got to this simple task, it felt like a burden. It felt like the last thing in the world a woman wanted to do...stand over a hot stove at the end of a long day, after doing every damn thing else. Ethic didn't require her to do anything but love him, so she had the desire and the energy to pour her soul into this meal. It wasn't a duty, it was an honor, to feed him because he fed her all day...her spirit...her soul...God, the ways that man kept her heart full. She told herself she would never not feed his in return. She swiped a joyful tear from her face and suddenly any notion of discomfort about being in his space was erased. She was right where she belonged. She didn't know why she had to go through everything she had been through to find herself in this place, but she knew it was purpose driven. God didn't make mistakes. The reason just hadn't been discovered yet. God's plan was so intricately designed, that she couldn't keep up, but as long as it involved this man and this love she found herself swept up in, she didn't care. Even after all the pain they had been through, she still wanted him.

She looked up, feeling another presence in the room. Morgan stood in the entryway, leaning against the wall. She was freshly showered, with wet hair pulled into a bun on top of her head. Sad eyes met Alani's.

"Can you hand me the olive oil?" Alani asked, with a sympathetic smile.

Morgan sighed and drug her feet across the tile to reach into a cabinet to retrieve it.

"Pour a bit over this," Alani instructed. Morgan did and then Alani nodded for the refrigerator. "Can you grab an onion and dice it, please?"

Morgan moved without protest. Alani expected some resistance but, surprisingly, she received none.

"Cooking is good for a broken heart. It requires love," Alani said.

"Only if you're good at it," Morgan replied. "I burn everything, so I must cook with hate."

Alani giggled at that.

"You want to learn?" Alani asked.

Morgan shrugged. "What's the point? I ain't got a man to cook for."

"The point is you have to eat," Alani returned, chuckling. "And when you do get a man, he'll appreciate the skill."

Morgan released a heavy sigh. "Why not?" she surrendered. She sniffed and wiped a tear, but another came, then another. Morgan gripped the countertop and lowered her head in grief. "I had a really good man. He was so good and then out of nowhere he wasn't. How could he lie like this?"

Alani washed her hands and then dried them, quickly, before going to Morgan.

"Oh, Morgan," she whispered. She lifted her face and wiped away Morgan's tears.

"I loved his mean-ass," Morgan whispered.

Alani smiled through sadness.

"You are a lovely girl. This is not your loss. It's his. He'll realize it; and when he does, the ball will be in your court. He better hope you're still interested in all that bad boy finesse he has; because if you ask me, you deserve more, Mo. Bad boys are only fun for a little while. You eventually outgrow them. Come on. Help me finish dinner before Ethic gets home. I can almost guarantee your talk will go smoother if he's not hungry."

Morgan nodded and followed Alani's lead. Her heart was on the floor and being trampled on. Nothing could distract her from that, but Alani was trying; and although Morgan wasn't fond of her, she appreciated the effort. It was motherly, and it was something Morgan hadn't felt in a long time. She hated that it came from someone she didn't want to mother her at all.

CHAPTER 8

The sports bar was empty, uncharacteristically quiet for a Saturday night. Ethic entered the darkened space and surveyed his surroundings, locating the back exit. A habit, from his time in the streets. Pool tables and television monitors filled the space. The college football game was on the screen. Nyair sat at the bar, hunched over it, as he nursed a drink in his hands - whiskey.

Ethic's expensive Gucci loafers announced him, as he made his way across the hardwood floor.

"Ethic," Nyair greeted, as he extended a hand for a handshake, rounding his fists to bring Ethic in for a brief connection before letting go.

Nyair called the bartender with a lifted finger and a pretty brunette bounced down to serve him.

"You drinking, bro?" Nyair asked.

"I didn't expect you to drink," Ethic answered, honestly. "The whole pastor thing and all."

"I'm a man of God, not perfection. I have a drink every now and then," Nyair answered.

"I'll take Hennessey, VSOP," Ethic ordered.

"You got it, handsome," the woman answered.

"I was surprised you picked this place. It's normally chaos on a Saturday night," Ethic said.

"Bought it out for a few hours. It's a low-key joint to enjoy the games and chop it up," Nyair said.

Ethic nodded.

He was taking notes in his head. What type of money did a pastor make to be able to buy out a popular sports bar for a casual meeting of the minds?

"I know who you are, Ethic. Benny Atkins' old shooter," Nyair said. "I thought you'd appreciate the privacy."

Ethic tensed, and the bartender returned, delivering his drink. Ethic placed his fingers over the top of the short tumbler and spun it in a circle. He didn't confirm nor deny. He just listened. Stupid men talked. Smart men listened. Sometimes, defense was the best offense. Nyair had the details mixed up. Ethic hadn't been Benny's shooter. He was Benny's connect, but the streets always told the story wrong. Ethic always let them.

"I came up in the city, running the streets, even tried my hand at Raven Atkins back in the day. She shot me down like only Raven Atkins can shoot a man down. Ego was on the floor, bro, but she was the dream. Every dude on the block wanted to shoot their shot. She loved only one, though. Claimed to be his girl, before he even knew she was throwing his name around. When I came at her, she said, *'Is your name Ethic? Cuz Ethic is the only nigga in this city that will ever be able to call me his girl.'* Then, she linked up with Mizan. Real bad dude. I was sorry to hear about what happened to her," Nyair said.

Raven's name amidst the conversation had Ethic sour. He knew she had been popular. Raven was Raven. The princess of the city, in her era, and everybody knew it. She wore a crown everywhere she went and made niggas kiss the ring whenever she felt like showing off. She was much like Morgan. Entitled. Which is why Ethic tried his hardest to keep Morgan removed from the very streets that had destroyed Raven.

"It was a long time ago, man," Ethic said, sweeping his reputation under the rug, as if it were no big deal.

"Seems that way," Nyair said, as he took a sip of his drink. "But Raven is a wound for you, bro. If you never heal from her, you go around bleeding all over every woman you encounter after her…including Alani."

Ethic's mind was blown.

That one concept had evaded him for years and Nyair brought it up so casually that Ethic knew he didn't realize how profound it was. Ethic had been walking around leaking his pain on everyone. Women. Hurting them. Torturing himself about something he couldn't change. He hadn't moved on at all. He was stuck in the past at that park, that tragic day that Raven had been shot.

"I don't want to punish her. I don't want to do anything but love her. I don't know if I know how to do that correctly. I've already hurt her too much," Ethic answered.

"Yeah, but you didn't know Alani before, man" Nyair said. "She's changed since meeting you. It's been a hard year for her, but before all this, she was just floating, man. I would be talking to her and her body would be there, but her mind would be on autopilot, just saying what she had to say and doing what she had to do to make people think she was present. She was unhappy. Miserable, in fact. I worried a lot about her, before you. I know she lost Kenzie and that's been hard, but she's feeling something again. She's living. She wasn't doing that for a long time, before you."

Ethic sipped his drink, as he pondered on the grand scheme of things. He could relate to the autopilot syndrome. He had done it for years. Was hurt necessary to peel away years of just going through the motions? Did it take something as drastic as losing children to break the locks that they both had put on their hearts? Now, it was open, and the pain was coming in, but so was the love...their love for one another. It was flowing freely, and they felt both.

"The pain will heal, and when it does, she'll only be able to feel whatever you're providing. Make sure you're healed by then, so that you'll be supplying love. When she touches you, you want her to feel divinity. You want her to experience a buzz so potent it gets her high, you feel me?" Nyair answered. Ethic's brow creased, as he wondered if Nyair had read his fucking mind because he did, in fact, feel every single thing that was coming out of Nyair's mouth.

"She wants to date," Ethic scoffed, surprising himself by opening up. "I'm trying to marry her and put a baby in her and she wants me to take her to the fucking movies, man."

"Put a baby in her at the movies. Get her pregnant before them credits roll, bruh," Nyair said, snickering. This was banter between men. It felt friendly and it was odd for Ethic because he had never had a right-hand.

He moved alone. Brotherhood didn't exist in his life. He had workers, shooters, young kings that looked up to him, Messiah wanting to follow in his footsteps, but never a friend. He was such a lone soul that he had never connected to another male in that way. No best friend growing up. No one to stand beside him as his best man, if the day ever came.

Ethic chuckled at the remark, as Nyair raised his glass and Ethic tapped it with his own.

"That for damn sure ain't preacher talk," Ethic said, with a shake of his head.

"Nah, but for real, man. I think Alani is right. Don't rush into it. What you rushing for? She isn't going anywhere. You got her. Take the time to get to know her and build a foundation that won't fall. That way when it's rocky, y'all don't break," Nyair added.

"So, date her," Ethic said, clearly annoyed by the concept of something so trivial. He was trying to change her last name. The picking her up and dropping her off at a separate house of it all frustrated him.

"Date her. Remove sex from the equation and get into her mind. Her heart. See if the connection is as potent with some restraint," Nyair said.

"Celibacy?" Ethic asked, raising skeptical brows. With Alani, that would be self-induced torture. Being inside her, buried in her femininity, made Ethic feel blessed...it made him feel like the recipient of love, instead of always being the giver of it. Alani made him calm. She made his heart feel safe. She was peace. His peace. He didn't know if he could not touch her. That type of restraint would take a miracle; but in order to become acquainted with the other parts that made up her person, he would try.

"Tell me about your moms."

Ethic removed his jacket and lifted from his seat. "I'ma need another round for that," he admitted. He finished his drink and then motioned for the brunette to bring him another. "You shoot?" Ethic asked, as he nodded toward the pool table.

Nyair lifted and took his libations with him to the table. Ethic racked the balls and then grabbed a pool stick. He chalked the tip.

"You can break," Ethic said. "So, you're a ball player. I'm assuming stick?"

"Running back. Football saved me from selling dope," Nyair admitted. "Went pro, made hella money, made some choices that ruined my career, lost a good woman, had to drown myself in my faith before I lost my mind."

"Pro? You must have been a beast on the field," Ethic said.

"I'm a beast everywhere," Nyair said. "It's just in my nature. I dominate. The football field, women, in business, in the church. Whatever I zone in on, I excel at. That's why I knew if I kept selling dope I was either going to be a kingpin or go to jail. That's how I knew your background. I worshipped your hustle coming up, bro."

"That's too bad," Ethic replied. "It's a trap. Once you're in it, it poisons you. Even after you're out. Glad you got out before it swallowed you whole."

"Seems like you were swallowed whole before that...what

did she do to you?" Nyair asked, pulling the conversation right back around to Ethic's mother.

Ethic tensed, as he watched Nyair take his shot.

Ethic leaned over the table, taking his time, because you just didn't rush or demand answers from a man like him. He closed one eye, as he pulled back the pool stick, then...

CLICK

"Corner pocket." One of the solid balls sank.

"She beat my ass and then she left. She was killed when I was seven. I ain't using that as an excuse. I'm a grown-ass man," Ethic said, giving him a less detailed version than he'd given to Alani.

"Hmm... nah, bruh, that's the heartbreak that did it. That moment she laid her first hand on you, she trained you that love comes with endurance. How much pain can you handle from the person you love? How much can you take? It never broke you as a child. You never stopped loving her, so your tolerance is high. You accept high levels of pain, so you give high levels of pain."

Ethic thought of Alani and something ached inside him. He had taken her through excruciation, just to get here, back at the beginning, back at movies and dinner. She was the one riding it out with him...enduring. Taking the hurt so that she could eventually get to the love. The realization of that made him feel low. It was a selfish expectation to have of your mate.

Damn.

"How do I break it? This bullshit cycle. She deserves nothing less than happiness. If I can't give her that…"

"You can't give her what you don't possess, G," Nyair said. He leaned over the table and banked one of the striped balls in a side pocket.

"I'll give her my all. Her and my kids. As long as they're happy, I don't need to have anything left over for me. I just want to do right by them," Ethic admitted. He picked up the tumbler and wet his lips with cognac. It warmed his entire chest on the way down. Ethic was a rare drinker, but this torment of pulling skeletons out of his closet intimidated him. He needed the liquid courage to even participate.

"And that's where you're messing up," Nyair said, pointing the entire pool stick at Ethic. He aimed, leaning, and CLICK. "Your shot," he told Ethic. He stood and placed both hands on his stick, as he continued. "You're pouring everything into the people you love. You're emptying your cup, bro. That leaves you weak, and if you're weak, how you supposed to protect them? How you supposed to love them? You want your cup to overflow. The cup sits in a saucer and it's overflowing it's so full. You go to God, talk to God, fill yourself up…you're so full that your saucer is catching the rest and you serve them from the overflow. It's so much to go around that your cup never empties. It's just overflowing with God's grace and His mercy and you giving all that to Alani, all that to Bella and your little man. You got to be full first."

"You say you know of me. You've heard things. The game was dirty. I played it for a long time. The things I've done…"

Ethic paused to clear his throat. "I can't take that to God and expect the same things He gives to you."

Nyair shook his head. "If my brother sins, rebuke him. If he repents, forgive him. It doesn't matter what you did before. I can see the remorse. The guilt. It hangs on you. It fills the air when you walk into the room. You're a different man now. You go to God with that. You put all that on the alter. You get on your knees and give it away and it'll never weigh on you like that again. God forgives His children, bro. I'm living proof of that."

"You're a football star," Ethic said. "I'm a gangster. Two different levels of sin."

"Nah, G. I ain't perfect. We all have the things we don't share. We all have the chapter in the book of our lives that we don't let others read," Nyair said.

"I doubt it measures up..."

"I killed a girl." The words were barely a whisper off Nyair's lips.

Silence. Not because Ethic was appalled. He had killed. He had sent more than a few to their graves, but he would have never pegged Nyair as the type.

"It's how I lost my contract. I got behind the wheel drunk. Me and my lady. She told me to let her drive. I thought I was fine. I was doing 120 up the highway, in a brand-new Lambo, in the middle of winter. Just stupid. Flashy. I hit a curve, there was ice on the road. The car flipped six times. She wasn't wearing a seat belt. She was tossed through the windshield. Died instantly. I was hit with vehicular manslaughter. I did four years."

Ethic's entire body steeled, as his eyes fell to the glass that sat on the side of the pool table.

"It's ginger ale," Nyair said. "I just wanted you comfortable. I can drink. Religion doesn't stop me from drinking. I just don't. Guilt stops me from taking even a sip. So, I know the things that God is capable of forgiving. It took me a long time to get to that point. So, I hold no judgements about where you come from or what you've done. When you kill the girl you love, that shit sticks with you."

Ethic's stomach plummeted. He knew about that. He felt that. He had lived with the anguish of that mistake for years... seven, to be exact. Part of him wondered if Nyair had made the entire thing up to relate to him, but he knew there was no way for him to know. Alani didn't even know. No one knew but him and it was something that caused him to lose sleep at night. He had loved Raven with his all, even before he had allowed himself to show it. He remembered sitting outside her house, at her father's request, watching the block, making sure things were safe and seeing her sneaking around with Mizan. It had burned him. He had wanted to kill Mizan, just from jealousy alone. If he had, Raven would still be alive. She had just been so young...off limits. She was the daughter of a man he respected, and it just didn't feel right to push up on her, but he had wanted to. With everything in him, he desired her. She had a lot of growing to do. She had been beautiful but so spoiled, so arrogant, and he had decided to let her flourish...let her live a little before he took her off the market. He had wanted her to grow up just a bit and then he had planned to make her his. There was a night when he had almost crossed the line. The first time she had slept under his roof, after the shooting at Morgan's birthday party. She had come to him in the middle of the night. Ethic had been so pent up with longing for her that he had to sweat it out. She had found him in his basement, lifting weights; and as soon as he had seen her face, his dick begged him to fuck her. Justine Atkins and Morgan had been upstairs, however, and if he parted her thighs, he knew she would be loud, so he didn't. So, he rejected her. He tried to be an honorable man and respect Benny Atkins enough not to knock down his daughter, but she was so fucking pretty. The prettiest girl he had ever seen. Still, to this day, no one was prettier. Morgan came close and that's why he kept her removed from the game. Raven had been a trophy and he had wanted her to sit shotgun next to him, his hand on her thigh, as niggas gawked at the sight of them...new king, new queen of the streets. He had been young then. His goals had been childish, his motivation had been money. She was the baddest and he was the richest. That, alone, meant they belonged together. He knew he would marry her one day, then Mizan wrapped Raven around his finger so tightly that things destructed before Ethic ever had a chance to make it right. Raven had never gotten the chance to grow into the woman he knew she would become, and it haunted him. She was supposed to be in her early 30's by now, raising their children, an entire gang of them because the type of love they made, seeds weren't to be wasted. She was supposed to be present to guide Mo. Perhaps, she would be running a business, if she wanted, but only if she wanted because there was no doubt in his mind that she would still be bourgeoise. He could see her living and breathing when he closed his eyes at night. She was supposed to be here, but she was gone and now he had Alani. He hadn't allowed his mind to process the tug of guilt he felt behind that yet. Ethic was moving on without Raven, and what he felt for Alani was so strong that it made him feel like he was betraying the girl that was supposed to be his forever. He had found a new forever. It felt like a life raft had been thrown to him, while he was struggling in the middle of a tumultuous ocean, but still, there was guilt. Ethic's eyes failed him, as they accumulated burden in the form of tears.

"You ever feel her? With you? Like when you first wake up, you almost hear her voice, but then you shake the fog off and remember she's not there?" Ethic asked. He was sick. Nothing about opening this can of worms felt good. He had kept it sealed for so long. If it weren't for Alani, he would have never pulled it off his shelf, but in order to keep her, he had to explore these emotions. He had to forgive himself. Unleash the hurt so he wouldn't hurt her. It felt like he was breaking bones. Like, in order for things to heal properly, he had to fuck them up more, break things down, before he could piece them back together. It hurt so fucking bad. He was almost angry at Alani for pushing him to do this because he wasn't ready.

"Every day since it happened," Nyair said. "Every fucking day, man."

Ethic had to bite back his emotion. Nyair definitely was no ordinary pastor. He was just a man. One that Ethic could relate too. One he could talk to without retribution. They were two, black men who had made mistakes that had cost them dearly, and Ethic had a feeling that Nyair would be the person to steer him out of the darkness. Finally.

CHAPTER 9

Whoa! Uncle Messiah, what happened to your car?" Saviour's voice traveled through the front door before he even opened it, as he yelled from the front yard. Messiah sat at Bleu's kitchen table, hands planted on the sides of his head, dread seizing his chest, as Bleu sat across from him. Bleu stood from the table, as the front screen door opened, and then slammed and Saviour came rushing into the kitchen.

"Hey, Mom!" he greeted, running right by her and into Messiah, who now stood too. Messiah picked up the little boy, feigning joy, although the sight of little Saviour did put a bit of life back into him.

"What up, boy? You knocking out them fucking books at school? You still doing your reading challenge?" Messiah asked, as he lifted the boy into the air, effortlessly, spinning him and then holding him upside down by the ankles.

"Yep! I've got the best reading grade in class! Agh! Mom, help! Help!"

Messiah shook Saviour. "Run them pockets, homie. I want all the nickels and dimes in there," Messiah teased, causing the change Saviour had in his jeans to spill onto the floor.

"Hey! That's mine! I collected it all at school. Found it fair and square!" Messiah put him down and went into his pocket and pulled out a knot of bills, peeling off one for Bleu's son.

"Here you go, boss," Messiah said.

"A hundred bucks! Thanks, Uncle Messiah!" Saviour said.

"You a man. You don't scrape for change, little homie, you play for the big bucks. Keep doing good in school, a'ight?" Messiah said.

"A hunnid dollars? Oh, you can pay a bill, then, young man," Bleu teased.

"Nigga, you don't pay bills in this bitch," Messiah griped. "Let nephew live."

"Messiah, your mouth! The boy already growing locs, so he can be like you. You gon' have him going to school talking cash shit!" Bleu exclaimed.

"Nah, he get that from his mama."

The voice came from Iman, as he strolled into the house. Bleu hit him, playfully, and Messiah nodded to Iman. The pair slapped hands. "What up, boy?" Messiah greeted.

"Not a thing, but from the looks of that windshield, you look like you got a lot of pieces moving on that chessboard over there," Iman stated.

Messiah scratched the back of his neck and grimaced. "It's complicated, bruh," Messiah stated.

"You love her?" Iman asked.

Bleu raised her hands, in surrender. "I'm going to go check to see if Saviour has homework."

She walked out the room and Messiah leaned against the center island, folding his arms across his chest.

"Nigga, go get your girl," Iman said, as he headed out of the kitchen.

"Yo, that's all you got? No words of wisdom on how to fix this shit?" Messiah said, dumbfounded, expecting more.

"I'm still trying to get my girl. The blind can't lead the blind, but I can tell you this. The further you let her get away from you, the harder it'll be to ever get that old thing back," Iman said. "That was the biggest mistake I could have ever made," Iman said. "Letting Bleu figure out she was better without me. Now, a nigga scraping and fighting to get her to lower that guard again. Don't miss your window trying to keep your G up. The streets can't love a nigga back."

Messiah sat in his BMW, curbside, a pistol resting in his lap, as he checked his side mirror, scanning the block... waiting. For Ethic. He saw Ethic's Range pull into the black gates that surrounded his home and Messiah hopped out the car, tucking his pistol in his waistline, as he hustled to catch the gate before it closed.

He could do it. Right then and there. Put a bullet in the back of Ethic's head, avenge Mizan, and walk off into the night. He could, but he couldn't because of her. The part of him that hated to give into sentiments was resistant to admit that even if Mo wasn't in the picture, he would still fail to pull the trigger. He respected Ethic, but a lot of disrespect had been going on lately, and Messiah was tired of moving in the shadows.

"Ethic…"

Ethic reached for his waistline, out of pure instinct, but when he turned to find Messiah, he relaxed. Messiah saw the malice leave Ethic's eyes, instantly. Complete trust.

"I take it you ready to have that talk you and Mo been avoiding for months?" Ethic asked. His jaw locked, and Messiah wished that was the only talk that was overdue. He felt like he was standing in front of his older brother, getting ready to be chewed out over a bad decision. Mizan had never given him this feeling…that he cared. Bookie had certainly never given him this feeling. Of fatherhood. Of family. He had been obligated to them out of duty. The blood flowing through his veins had been like chains, bonding him, enslaving him, indebting him to two men who had hurt him more than anyone in the world. The things they had done to him. The irreversible damage they had done…the ways they had hindered him…he was angry because what they had made him into would make it hard for him to love Mo the way she deserved. He fought against his very nature just to give her what he did. Just to open up to her, it took more than she could ever know.

"You know?" Messiah asked.

Ethic reached into his backseat and pulled out a bouquet of fresh lilies.

Messiah eyed them and grasped his wrists in front of his body.

"You get a woman to put up with your bullshit, you make sure you bring flowers home," Ethic stated.

Messiah felt his gut hollowing and his eyes misted. *What the fuck?* He thought, as he sniffed away the emotion. He had been there, watching Ethic through the years of torment, through the loneliness, and now Ethic had a woman…had earned a woman. Ethic wasn't pulling up to an empty house, but to one where his woman waited for him inside.

"It's my job to know every piece on my chessboard, Messiah. I taught you that. I suppose this is my fault. Expecting you to be around Mo, protect her, be there when I couldn't…she's a splitting image of her sister. I know what that temptation feels like. Feels like you're willing to die behind that risk."

Ethic deadpanned on Messiah, eyes flickering in anger, but Messiah met his stare because he was a man…Ethic had taught him how to be a man and men looked niggas in the eye without falter. "You just might die behind that, little nigga. Come on in. I'm sure Alani cooked. I'll have her set you a plate, so you and Mo can tell me all the reasons why I shouldn't fucking kill you," Ethic stated.

He put a firm palm on the back of Messiah's neck and steered him toward the house.

There it was. Unconditional love from a man…from family, and Messiah felt like folding. He had seen Ethic ride out over Mo. He remembered the nigga who had lost three fingers for whistling at Mo when she was 14 and walking out of the gas station. Ethic had shot them off in broad daylight, without thinking twice. To be cognizant of their affair all this time and not act against Messiah meant he was family. His face contorted in pain because he was about to lose his family. Ethic's back was toward Messiah, as he placed his key in the door. Messiah melted down, battling back and forth in his mind how to hide this secret, how to maintain his world, but Wozi was in town, no way could he continue the façade. The ultimatum had been set. Clip Ethic or Morgan became the new target.

"You're not who I want for Mo. Your lifestyle isn't what I want for Mo, but Mo wants it for herself. She wants you and I've always given her what she wanted. If that's you, you got to know that this street shit is a wrap...you got to-"

"This ain't about Mo..."

The way his voice cracked caused Ethic to turn around, in stun. He lifted hands of surrender, sending the flowers crashing to the ground. The vase broke into pieces at his feet, as he stared down the barrel of Messiah's gun.

A milli-second of hurt filled Ethic and then it was gone and replaced with rage.

"Even the smallest pawn can kill the king if he's not paying attention," Ethic muttered to himself, shaking his head and scoffing. He flicked his nose and clenched his jaw, as a contemptuous stare fell onto Messiah. "You pulled it now, now you got to bang with it, because if you won't, I will. One of us is dying tonight."

Messiah's lip quivered but his aim was steady, as anguish filled his eyes.

"You've been around me for a long time, Messiah. You know what comes next, so you might as well pull the trigger.

Leave me on my doorstep for Mo to find, for Eazy, for Bella," Ethic sneered.

"I was a kid when you pulled up on me in Gundry Park." Messiah stated. "You the first mu'fucka in my whole fucked-up life that ever did something for me, without fucking me over first." He swiped one hand down his face to rid himself of the emotion that threatened to spew out of him. He hadn't expected this...to feel like this...the conflict... the remorse...Messiah was the type of nigga that pulled triggers and then went about his way like nothing had even occurred. Pulling this trigger was a task, however. It felt weighted.

Ethic stepped up, so that the barrel of the gun was pressed into his chest.

"Nah, nigga. Don't reminisce. Don't tell me how I used to feed you, clothe you, teach you how to piss straight, how to shoot straight. Pull the fucking trigger." Ethic's voice was void of affection and it was so low it was almost a whisper.

The front door opened.

"Ethic!" Alani's voice behind him pulled at him, but he didn't turn.

"Go in the house," Ethic stated, without looking at her. He saw Messiah's eyes shift to the door and Ethic knew Morgan had stepped out onto the porch before he ever heard her. He could see her presence affect Messiah, weaken him.

"What are you doing...Messiah?"

It was the split second needed for Ethic to react. He rushed Messiah, grabbing his wrist with the gun with one hand and wrapping a strong hand around Messiah's neck with the other. With ribs still tender from being shot, it took all his strength to turn Messiah, pinning him against the house. The power of the punch Ethic delivered to Messiah's body folded him, as Ethic removed the gun from Messiah's possession. Burner to the head, malice in his eyes, Messiah knew it was his day to die.

Ethic's forearm was at his throat, keeping him hemmed, and tears fell from his eyes. He only knew what they were because he had felt them before, the night he thought Mo had been killed. It had been his first introduction to crying. This time, his tears would be his goodbye.

"Tell me why I shouldn't blow your head off," Ethic sneered. "I know this ain't about money, it ain't about power, so what the fuck is it about, Messiah?"

Messiah's face sneered, as he tried to control his emotion, but his teeth chattered with the quaking of his chin, his lips curling up, staring Ethic in the eyes. Not an ounce of fear lived in him, only remorse, but he was a man. He held his head high, as he looked Ethic in his eyes, with no waver.

"Ethic!" Morgan cried. "Ethic, please, no!" Morgan was on pins and needles, standing to the side, watching the two men she loved most go to war. This was her fault. She knew it. She had known all along it would come to this.

Alani stood with her hands, praying over her mouth. "Baby, don't...Ethic...please..."

"You got to the count of three," Ethic stated.

Messiah would rather Ethic pull the trigger than let the words fall from his mouth.

"One," Ethic counted. "Two…"

"No…no…no…no…please," Morgan pleaded. "Ethic, I'm…"

Before she could let the word pregnant roll off her pretty tongue, Messiah rolled his head to the side, looking her in the eyes and said, "Mizan is my brother."

The words collided with Morgan, knocking her off balance, as she reached one hand out for Alani and crumbled into her arms. Her sobs filled the air, as she panicked. Ethic felt like he couldn't breathe, as confusion played in his eyes. He had vetted Messiah. He had known him since he was a young kid, walking around with tattered clothes, an empty stomach, and fresh bruises. How had he missed this?

"Take Mo inside," Ethic said, without looking at Alani.

"Ethic, no! No, I can't do that," Alani protested. "If you're going to pull that trigger, you'll have to do it with me standing here. You know what that'll do…you know, Ethic, please, baby, don't do this."

"Why the fuck do you little niggas like to play with me? Mizan's fucking brother," Ethic scoffed, sickening more and more by the second. He was so close to Messiah that Messiah could smell the cognac on Ethic's breath and see the red in his maddened eyes, as the tattooed forearm choked the life from him. "I raised you." He struggled against Ethic, but the power behind Ethic's hold, the rage acting as motivation, the deceit fueling his every movement, made it impossible to counter his strength. "I put money in your pocket and food in your stomach…" Ethic tapped the gun at Messiah's temple. "…fucking knowledge in your simple-ass head and this is what the fuck you got to say to me? This is what you do?"

Messiah grit his teeth, scrunching his face in pain, as those tears he was fighting rushed him, washing to the surface like a wave, taking him under, pulling him with the tide… drowning him.

"I just want to belong somewhere, man. I just want to be here with her," Messiah whispered.

"Ethic…"

Alani's voice was so weak and so pained that Ethic closed his eyes. He had heard these pleas before. When she had begged him to let Cream live. He had done it and it had been the biggest mistake of his life. Cream had come back one day. His humanity, extended because she had asked him to spare a life, had led to the destruction of his child…of Love. So many scenarios ran through his head. Messiah had been trained by him, bred up by him, to be a killer, to be a hustler, to outwit the opposition…now he was the opposition. There was no letting a nigga like that walk. He was dangerous. He was Mizan's brother and all these years, he had been smart enough to hide it. Ethic played the years back in his mind. Messiah had been by his side every step of the way, as he searched for Mizan. Somehow, Mizan had always outrun him, had always escaped…Ethic always narrowly missed catching up to him, until the one time he kept Messiah out of the loop. *This nigga was warning him…*

Ethic had taken Messiah to New York with him as backup in a huge deal with a longtime supplier he worked with. Mizan happened to be there and Ethic had made his move on Mizan, without hesitation. Messiah didn't even know the murder had gone down until after it was too late. *His fucking brother,* Ethic thought. *Why the fuck was he around before I even clipped Mizan? He's been around since he was a fucking kid,* Ethic recounted. Ethic remembered being just a teen when he'd pulled up on Messiah at a bus stop. It had been freezing cold in the middle of winter and he wore not coat. He had on a raggedy, little button-down shirt and had tucked his head inside the collar to stay warm. Raggedy sneakers with exposed soles had graced his feet. Ethic had pulled off his First Down goose jacket, without hesitation, and offered the kid a ride. Messiah had declined but he accepted the coat. The next day when Ethic had ridden by, he had a pair of shoes for Messiah. They had been mentor and mentee ever since, big brother, little brother...family ever since...only they weren't because Mizan was Messiah's family and anybody affiliated with Mizan was no friend of Ethic's. A mole for Mizan was a threat. One that needed to be eliminated immediately.

"I can't...God, Alani, I just can't breathe. I can't do this," Morgan cried, rushing into the house. Alani was torn between going after Morgan and staying at Ethic's side. She feared going inside and hearing the gun go off. She knew she wouldn't...she couldn't...be with him if he did this again. He was supposed to be growing, changing. Murder couldn't be the answer for everything. Could it? Was this really what his world was like? Full of treachery and danger? The stakes were always so high in Ethic Land. Was it ever normal? Ever easy?

"Be here with her? You want to be with her? After plotting on my family for years? After being around my kids. I trusted you with them-"

As if he had spoken Eazy and Bella up, Lily pulled into the driveway.

"Get my kids in the house and lock the doors," he ordered, not even looking at Alani. She could hear the malice in his tone...see the possibility of consequence dancing in his eyes. His stare was deadly, and he had marked Messiah as the target. He pulled Messiah off the brick wall and pushed him toward his Range, making sure to tuck the gun in his waist, so his children didn't see it.

"Messiah!" Eazy called, as he hopped out the car in excitement. "I've got to show you my new game! It's so cool!"

Eazy ran toward Messiah, but Alani quickly grabbed him, intercepting him.

"Let your daddy talk to Messiah, okay? Let's get in the house. You can show me the game," Alani said. She tried her hardest to conceal the quiver in her voice. "Come on, B." Alani ushered them both toward the house.

"Next time, homie," Messiah stated, his voice doomed with sadness because he knew there would be no next time.

"Get in the car," Ethic ordered, pointing to the driver's side. Messiah took a deep breath because he knew where they were headed. He didn't even have to ask, as he backed out the driveway and headed to Devil's Lake.

"So put the shit together for me," Ethic scoffed, as he pulled the gun and rested it in his lap, hand curled on the trigger...ready.

"My father is Bookie Grant. He never claimed me. Williams is my mother's last name," Messiah said.

Ethic knew who Bookie was. An old enemy of Benny Atkins. He had heard the name before. A woman beater. He used to lay hands on his wife so badly that she came running to Justine Atkins for help. Justine went to Benny. Benny had eyes and ears in the local police precinct and when he got word that Bookie's spot was under surveillance, he let Bookie go down. It was where the resentment between Bookie and Benny began.

They both knew the history. Ethic just didn't know that Benny had another son…that Messiah was his second son, birthed out of wedlock.

"When I met you, there was nothing to it. You were my big homie. You looked out. I knew you for years before any funny business ever went down. Then, Mizan targeted Raven. Targeted her for a long time, way before she even knew he existed. He used to sit outside her school, with me in the car, watching her for hours. He said that she was the way to get payback on Benny Atkins. Turn her out and then kill her. That was his plan. I didn't want to. I wasn't with that shit. I was making money with you by that point, and I was just trying to get my weight up, but then you left town, after Benny Atkins' funeral you just got ghost and I had to eat. I ain't have no connect, so I got work from my brother. He would show me pictures of her all beat up, all slapped up, bragging about how he kept his hoes in line. I wasn't with it, though, but she wasn't my business."

Messiah pulled into the deserted area and Ethic motioned for him to get out the car, gun aimed.

"Then, she broke free of that nigga. Left town with you; and no lie, this nigga went crazy. He was obsessed over finding her. When Raven came back to Flint, he tied her up in his basement like a dog. Had her eating off the floor and shit, man. Next thing I know, she's dead and Mizan's on the run, then you came back to town. You put me up on so much game and I ain't talking about street shit. You told me to develop an exit plan. Taught me about money, about looking a nigga in his eyes when I speak. I didn't have that before you. Bookie used to beat the shit out of me, lock me in closets, in the garage on the hottest days of summer. The air would be so thick I couldn't breathe. I kept asking my mama why she wouldn't help me...why he would hit me so hard that it felt like my chest would cave in, and she kept saying he just wants to make sure I became a man," Messiah scoffed. "That he didn't want me to be like him. I was a kid, man. I didn't understand until one day I walked home from school early because I was sick. I walked in on him getting his dick sucked by a little kid, man. The little boy was my age. I recognized him from my school. He looked at me and told me I was next. I ran after that...I ran away from home and Mizan would look out for me. I stayed with him for a little while, but he wasn't with the baby sitting and I wasn't with begging. I bounced around a lot, until I met you and started getting money. Before that, I was terrified because he was my father and I thought the shit was in my veins...that I would grow up to be like him. A man who slept with other men and then beat his woman to keep her from telling anybody. When my pops got locked up, it was the happiest day of my life. When I found out how it was laying between you and Mizan, I said fuck Mizan. But when Bookie found out I was playing on your side, he told me to kill you. Told me to kill you or he would make sure his people on the outside killed me. Told me they would make a man out of me and put me on my knees like he had done that little boy I walked in on. He said blood was blood and that I wasn't a man if I didn't get payback for Mizan. I told him no and he sent niggas to my mama door. They killed her. Slit her throat so deep we had to have a closed casket. My sister, Wozi, came home to find her. If I didn't kill you, Wozi was next. There was only one condition. He wanted the name of your connect first. Your connect would be the leverage he used to get out of prison…"

"So, you waited years. You've been plotting for years. You're a patient nigga, Messiah," Ethic stated.

"I wasn't waiting for nothing. I had my reasons. I thought I'd die first out here and then your downfall wouldn't be on my conscience, but I'm still here. Still ticking," Messiah said. "Morgan gave me a reason to live because I know for a fact I was supposed to be out of here by now."

Messiah was spilling his soul, telling his darkest secrets. He was bouncing all over the place, jumping from childhood to his teenage years, making it hard for Ethic to discern what had happened when, but Ethic knew it was the nerves jumbling the timeline. Messiah was standing in front of death and that just did things to a man. Ethic had been on that ledge before, waiting to die, so he listened to this last testament without interrupting. Ethic was a father, so he knew how a man could have the power to manipulate his son. He knew it was easy for a man to invoke fear from his offspring and put doubt in their minds to get his way. Ethic had never been that type of parent. He never wanted his seeds to feel anything other than love from him. Niggas like Bookie were the worst type. He wondered if Messiah had left parts out. If Bookie had ever actually put Messiah on his knees…if he had ever made his son question his masculinity because Ethic could see the fear in Messiah's eyes, regarding that part. He had always wondered where Messiah's rage came from. Now, he knew. It was bottled up rage over the abuse he had endured. Ethic could relate to that. Ethic felt that. It had taken him a long time to detach himself from it and to realize that the sins of the father or the mother were not his own. Ethic pressed the gun to Messiah's forehead.

"I was never touching, Mo. I need you to make sure she knows. I was never going to hit the kids. I could barely do you. Even tonight, all it took was one finger curled on the trigger. They would be cleaning you up off the pavement right now, but I couldn't…everything I am that's worth something is built on what you put in me. I just want to belong to somebody, man. I just want her to love me. Not the nigga I try hard to be in front of her, but the one I was hiding from her. I've been hiding so much…that's it. That's my peace, O.G. Just get the shit over with."

Not an ounce of fear played on his face. He held his head high, as he looked at Ethic, in the eyes, no waver. A man had to stand behind the decisions he made, even on judgement day. A man who sniveled and cried and begged when things came to a head wasn't much of man at all. Messiah was all king. Not an ounce of bitch was a part of his make-up. The cat was out of the bag, so it was time to square up. All cash, no credit. "Just make sure she knows. I ain't say it enough, and now she won't hear it again and she's going to doubt a nigga. I love her. You tell her that for me."

Ethic wanted to lay Messiah down for his trespass, but he couldn't reconcile the consequences of such in his head. Another black man would be gone at his hand. Black on black, wrong on wrong. Did Messiah's ill deeds justify Ethic's? He knew they didn't. He knew if he ended Messiah, a young man he had loved once upon a time, it would affect him. It would smear his soul and Ethic just wanted his hands to be cleansed of all they had done, all the triggers he had pulled. Ethic couldn't seek redemption and turn around and do something like this. He grit his teeth, angry at himself, at Messiah. He pressed that steel gun into the center of Messiah's forehead, sneering in angst as he shouted, "Arghh!"

Ethic lowered the weapon and pulled Messiah into him by the back of the neck, hugging him, as Messiah broke down on Ethic's shoulder. Two, grown men, crying over what they knew was a bond lost and an undeserving life saved.

Ethic pulled back first and sniffed away his emotion, as he put the gun in his waistline.

"Stay away from Mo. Stay out of Flint."

Ethic turned and walked away. His soul and his heart told him that he had done the right thing. His mind spoke differently. He only hoped that he wouldn't live to regret it.

CHAPTER 10

A lani sat at the kitchen table, her dainty fingers spinning the stem of the wine glass, as the red cabernet tornado spun inside. She was in a daze, as the hours ticked by on the clock. The house was still. The sounds of Morgan crying through the closed door upstairs had finally ceased, conquered by exhaustion and the kids were down for bed. Alani couldn't sleep. Her heart wouldn't let her. *Three in the fucking morning,* she thought, as she checked her phone in frustration. It had been a long time since she had stayed up all night worried about the comings and goings of a man. Cream had taken her through it countless times, and all those combined hadn't felt as bad as this. Something much greater was at stake. She lifted the wine glass to her dry lips. Wine always dried her lips, for some reason; probably, because she always paired it with tears. Red wine and crying just went together. *702,* pumped through the speakers, as Alani bobbed her head to the sad song.

You know I don't want to stayyy
You know I don't want to goo
Baby, please, listen to me
I don't wannaaaaa

It was on repeat and she closed her eyes because she felt those lyrics in her soul. She feared the worst. If Ethic killed Messiah, her darkest reservations would be realized. That, yes, he was in fact a killer and that her daughter hadn't been some unfortunate mistake, but that murder was a habit of his…if that was the case, how could she stay? But, damn, she wanted to stay. To love every single part of the gangster he kept hidden inside because when he let that inner G surface, it made her panties wet. The sound of the alarm rang out, letting her know he was home. Only the light above the stove was on. Everything else was off and it cast an eerie, yellow glow throughout the kitchen. Ethic took the house by memory, following the music to the island where she sat.

They squared off. Her in her seat, eyes burning him as soon as he entered the room. Him, standing, gripping the back of the chair across from her.

"Did you kill him?" Alani asked. "Because if you did…"

"You'll leave, Alani. I know…" He barked the words, taking a tone with her he'd never taken before…one of frustration, like she had put his back against the wall by asking him not to act with malice…like he was tired of her kum ba ya shit and just wanted to reveal his gangster. Alani was unaffected. She was a big girl. She could take whatever energy he had walked through the door with.

"No. Then, I'd love a killer and that would turn me into someone else. Someone I don't know. So, did you?"

"He's alive," Ethic said.

Alani breathed a sigh of relief for the first time in hours. Ethic placed his hands under her arm pits and lifted her out the chair, placing her on the bar.

He took her in, analyzed her, took his time…letting his eyes sweep over every inch of her face. Every last pore, every perfect imperfection. She was so fucking pretty. He didn't miss the black dress, sleek, pressed hair swept to the back, and maroon-painted lips and fully made face. She had waited for him in a black dress…the close to empty bottle of red wine next to her told him she had waited awhile. A woman in a black dress…a woman to call his own. The care behind the gesture spoke volumes. Alani placed one hand on the side of his face, the imperfect side, her caring eyes probing him. Ethic slid between her bare legs, pulling his shirt over his head, as he accosted her. He pulled her to the edge, black-ass fingers digging into the meat of her thighs, as he stepped out of his pants.

She didn't say one word. She just sat there, holding that wine glass in one hand, tilting it to her lips for one last sip before he relieved her of it.

"The kids are upstairs," she said.

"Fuck them kids," he growled, as he shed the boxer briefs next. He was strong. Veins bulging, skin stretched, lengthy and wide all at the same time. "I need to feel you cuz right now I don't feel shit, so you got to make me feel something, Lenika. Let me feel you, baby," he whispered, finessing her panties down her legs. He filled her with all the frustration, all the betrayal, all the angst that had numbed him. Alani's brown thighs parted, and she clenched her eyes tightly from the bliss of it all. Her mouth fell open, but he filled it, with his tongue, gripping the side of her face with one hand, before moving those lips to her ear and then down her neck. He never missed a beat, as he ravished her. Strong thighs made him thrust deeper. He had told her once...that he wanted to fuck her on this very countertop; now, here she was, being a ho and loving it.

She saw the turmoil in his eyes and she gripped his face, pausing for just a beat.

"Hey," she said. He froze, looking at her and she saw a void in him. He had lost something today. Messiah held value in Ethic's life. Alani could see the hole in him. "You don't have to be gentle. Let it out."

His next thrust was harder and Alani's back arched as she took it. He pulled her off the island all together, planting solid feet onto the kitchen floor, strong legs, holding up all her weight on bent thighs, as he bounced her down on his dick. He penetrated her just right, going so deep that Alani had to bite her lip to stop herself from moaning too loud. He carried her to the wall, resting her back against it, and she wrapped her legs around him, as he climbed further into her.

"Give it all to me, Ethic," she whispered, her face twisted in pain...in extreme pleasure...this had to be the devil's work. It felt too good to be God. It felt too good to be blessed. This shit was cursed. This dick would send her to hell; and as long as he was there, she didn't care. God, what had he done to her? There wasn't anything she wasn't willing to trade to be here with him, to have him in it, in her, like this, forever.

I don't really wanna stay
I don't really wanna go
But I really need to know
Can we get it together?

Repeat.

Alani came all over him, three times, the song looped eight before he had enough. Her body was spent. They were covered in sweat and heaving. Ethic fisted her hair and kissed her lips, while she ran her hands down the back of his head, soothingly. She just wanted to heal him. Cover those wounds the night had put on his heart because he was bleeding all over the place. He never disconnected their lips, as he wrapped both hands around her thighs, hoisting her up. He carried her toward the stairs, not caring that he was naked. In that moment, Alani didn't care either. He was the king of her heart, of this castle, of this city. He could walk around this bitch naked if he pleased. It was his shit. He had built it and he was offering it all to her. A kingdom for a queen. She had never quite seen herself in that light before, but she had been crowned by Ezra Okafor, so she had to be royal in some way...even if only one, for him to pick her. His chosen and she loved him.

He placed her on her feet and then wrapped arms around her. Their original form of connection. An embrace. The thing that put will into her legs when she had none. He needed this and she held onto him tightly.

"How's Mo?" he mumbled.

"Devastated," Alani whispered. "Completely devastated."

He pulled back and Alani sat on the bed, watching him, as he moved to the dresser to retrieve clothes. He took heavy steps back to her, and then leaned down to peck her lips. He was always kissing her when he departed, no matter how brief the disconnection, he always said goodbye. Even a trip to the next room came with a kiss on the cheek.

"I'm going to speak with Mo. Get some rest."

She closed her eyes and nodded, but no way would she be sleeping tonight. When he was unsettled she felt it. She always had from the day she had tried to live without him, his turmoil traveled through thin air, across miles and infected her. No way would one wall keep his energy away. She waited for him to close the door on his way out, then got down on her knees and put praying hands in front of her face. She closed her eyes and went to speak to God, because with all the pain festering beneath the roof of this house, she knew that He was the only entity capable of providing some relief.

The taste of salty tears lingered on Morgan's lips, as she spread her lips wide with grief, crying so hard that no sound came out. She lay on her side, her fist balled beneath her face, the other balled at her heart, gripping the cover. She couldn't breathe. Her chest was heavy, so heavy that pushing air into her lungs felt impossible. The burn in her swollen eyes was unbearable, but she couldn't close them because when she did she pictured him. Messiah. Mizan's brother. The door creaked open and Morgan didn't even look to see who was entering. She didn't care. If it wasn't Messiah coming to take back his admission of truth, nothing anyone else had to say would matter.

Ethic appeared before her eyes, kneeling in front of her bed, so that he was eye level with her. She heaved when they made eye contact. She crumbled. Crying so hard and so loud that he pulled her from the bed and onto the floor into his arms. Morgan was destroyed.

"Shh," he whispered, as he rubbed her hair, soothingly, and cradled her, rocking her gently like he used to do when she was a child, right after Raven had died. This felt like that... like death...like Messiah had died right in front of her... like she now had to put him in the ground and mourn his passing. In a sense, it was exactly that because what Morgan felt was pure grief. To love a man as potently as she had done with him and then to be blindsided by this truth was torture. Every memory they shared. Every touch he had gifted. Every kiss, each orgasm, was like a ghost coming back to haunt her.

She sat there in Ethic's arms, depleted. It took a full hour for her cries to dry up, not because the feeling lessened but because she ran out of tears. Her eyes were so red it looked like she was high. They were swollen and sore. She had never felt so low. So empty. Nausea swept over her, reminding her that she was with child and she crawled frantically toward the trash can next to her bed. Ethic was right behind her, on his feet, holding her hair out of the way as she let it all out.

"Is he dead?" Morgan asked.

She didn't know if she wanted the answer to be yes or no. She just needed information. More information. An explanation. A fucking diagram, some pictures, a flow chart, to tell her how she had ended up in the bed of Mizan's brother. How? How was he related to the one person who was single-handedly responsible for orphaning her?

"No, Mo. He won't be around anymore, though. You won't have to see him. He's been warned. You don't got to worry about that," Ethic whispered.

Morgan didn't know what she felt. There were so many emotions swirling around inside she felt combustible.

"You should sleep, Mo," Ethic said.

"I'll never be able to sleep again," she whispered to herself.

CHAPTER 11

One Week Later

Morgan rolled over onto her back, her eyes were still closed. It didn't even feel like she had slept. It had been a restless night...the past seven had been restless nights, in fact. A heaviness weighed down upon her. She reached out for him...but only emptiness existed next to her. She had forgotten just that quickly that he was gone. He had spent so many nights in her bed for months that they had developed a routine. The urge to cuddle beneath him in the morning was automatic for her. On this day, his side of the bed was cold and the space next to her felt infinite. The white sheets felt like an island that she was stranded on...deserted and alone...stretching for miles and miles...so far that no one could hear her screams for help. An ache settled into her stomach and she rolled wet eyes to the ceiling. Messiah was gone. There would be no coming back. There couldn't be. If he ever came around, Ethic would kill him. Ethic had wanted her to stay close to home for a while, but Morgan wanted to grieve in peace. She wanted to be in her apartment, where Messiah had once been because the smell of him still lingered. Ethic called every day,

FaceTimed twice a day to check on her. The one time she had activated her DO NOT DISTURB, he came racing up the highway to check on her and stayed all day, so that she could rest her head on his lap and cry. He had rubbed her hair gently and talked about old times with her father, just like he used to do when she was a little girl. Morgan just wanted to cry Messiah out her system. She needed to purge herself of the memories. She both loved and hated him. She was shattered. Images of her sister's face crept into her mind and her lip quivered. Messiah was Mizan's brother.

How did this happen? Morgan's entire family had fallen because of Mizan. She remembered a time before Raven had met him. The Atkins' had been happy. They had been safe and then Raven brought Mizan home one night and nothing was ever the same. Morgan remembered feeling the walls of her bedroom vibrating from Mizan throwing Raven against them when she was a child. She remembered the black eyes, the bruises, and the undoubtable fear that always lived in Raven's eyes. It had been an unbearable time. Mizan had never hurt her. He spoiled her, in fact, but the things he had done to her sister, it was enough to terrify Morgan. She had always feared making him angry because each time Raven had made him angry, he hurt her. Morgan had made sure she was perfect and absolutely silent...like white paint...she had just been a fixture in the home...something that you didn't even notice when you walked in. All to avoid Mizan's wrath. She had lived every day in absolute terror and then their mother died. It was the event that had caused Ethic to come back to town and rescue them. Tears rolled out of her eyes, soaking her pillow, as her chest heaved, and the white ceiling haunted her. It was like a projection screen, playing back her past. Mizan had been a monster. *And I just let his brother in the same way.*

Morgan was so angry she couldn't be angry. She was confused, distraught, in denial, and so incredibly hurt. The truth ate through her like a parasite, infecting her, sickening her, weakening her…Morgan was shattered. Messiah was her first love and the remnants of this heartbreak would be with her forever. It was the heartbreak that would teach her never to give 100 percent of herself ever again. She hadn't kept anything in reserve. Morgan had jumped into loving Messiah with every single fiber of her being. She had trusted him with it all and he had fumbled her. The foul on the play had injured her and now he was gone, and Morgan was ready to quit the game. She would never love another so fully again. A woman's first love determined how she loved for the rest of her life. The next man would catch hell because of the carnage Messiah had left behind. Men didn't understand the amount of culpability they took on when they kissed a woman beyond her lips. When that kiss infiltrated her soul and opened her aura, he had the power to build or break. Messiah had begun the process of constructing Morgan's womanhood. He had given her confidence and taught her to be brave. He had witnessed her evolution. He had encouraged her to be bold because she knew she had him in the background, watching her back, keeping her grass cut, and holding his arms wide in case she slipped. Messiah had started the blueprint to helping her become a better woman…a stronger woman.

Then, out of nowhere, she discovered he was fraudulent, and the letdown was catastrophic. She had already run up the tab on him and he couldn't repay the debt. It was like he had overextended his budget of love and had abandoned the expensive project that was her heart altogether. He hadn't finished the job and the breakdown of everything he had constructed was torture. Morgan imploded and the demolition of what she thought they were, what she had thought she meant to him, made her feel like dying. She felt every single chip, as all the lies he had told eroded her belief in him.

"A nigga who don't mean you no good could be staring you right in your face and you wouldn't know it until it's too late."

She remembered the words, vividly. *He was talking about himself. He was right...it's too late.*

Morgan peeled herself out of bed. She felt numb. She felt her feet against the plush carpet, as she made her way to the bathroom. Her eyes were not her own in the reflection. They were Raven's. She recognized this dismal heartbreak. She had memorized that look at the age of six. She remembered the fight she'd had with Messiah. She ran her thumb against the inside of her ring finger on her right hand. It had healed. The bones had healed but the altercation with Messiah had broken it in the first place. Knowing that he was Mizan's brother made Morgan question it all. She had gotten hurt. It had been an accident, or had it? She didn't know anymore. There had been so much rage inside of Messiah. Ever since she'd known him, he had been a menace. It was what had attracted her. She had wanted to tame him, to be the only one to manage that fury. Being the girl he loved enough to calm for was like a badge of honor. He found enough value in her to be still, but now... Knowing his anger was aimed at her family the entire time sent a chill down her spine. He had gotten so close. He was a threat and could have touched her or Bella or Eazy or Ethic at any moment. She recalled the day at Alani's when Messiah and Ethic had faced off. There had been so much ire in the air. The discovery that she never really knew Messiah was enough to bring her to her knees. She felt lonelier than before he had come into her life. At least before she hadn't known how good it felt to belong to someone. Now that she knew, the silence of misunderstanding was deafening. There wasn't a sign her fingers could portray that could help her voice this hurt. He had disabled her. Emotionally, she was handicapped beyond repair.

Messiah had broken her.

Morgan couldn't eat. She couldn't sleep. She couldn't think. She was just rotting. Messiah should have just left her frozen, because now that he had unthawed her, she was just going to waste. It was a sick notion to want to be healed by the very person whom had done the ailing, but she knew that no one would be able to take this ache away except Messiah. She picked up her phone and dialed him for the 100th time. Literally, call number 100. He hadn't answered any of the attempts before and it tore her up inside. Morgan didn't even want to speak to him. She hated him. She didn't trust him... couldn't trust him. She was terrified of him, but still, she had called repeatedly. There was something about knowing that she still had him on a string that would have made this easier, but he was refusing to answer. He was a ghost in her life…a memory, and Morgan couldn't manage the grief. She would rather be fighting with him, at war with him, than separated from him. There was something about the vigor he gave her…it didn't matter if they were on good or bad terms, it didn't matter if they were friend or foe…it was the exchange of energy that she craved. It was a necessity to breathe… to function…to feel significant. She had made the mistake of only seeing the value he gave her, and now that he was gone, her self-worth had plummeted. If she couldn't love him, she wanted to hate him, and she wanted him to know how much she hated him, but he was ignoring her. That only made it worse. Attention. She needed his attention and she was willing to do anything to get it.

The knock at Morgan's door was the only thing that reminded her that there was an entire world outside. She had been barricaded behind a wall of heartbreak for days. She took somber steps out her bedroom and into her living room before pulling open the door.

Aria stood in the hallway, face bent, in perplexity.

"What the fuck, Mo? Where have you been? Did you get my text about auditions?" she asked. "I've been calling you for days." Morgan's red eyes and disheveled exterior made Aria take pause. "What's wrong?"

"We're done. Messiah and I," Morgan whispered. "It's overrrr!" she wailed. Her face crushed in agony, as Aria stepped over the threshold and pulled her in for a hug.

"Oh, Mo," she whispered. "It's not over. Just give things time to cool down. I don't know who that bum was that he's messing with, but he loves you. I know he messed up but-"

Morgan pulled back, shaking her head, as she wiped her tears. "There are no buts. He's a liar. So many secrets. He told so many lies, Aria! I have so many questions...I'm so confused and I just need to know the truth. It's shit I can only hear from him, but he won't answer my calls!"

"Fuck that. He owes you an explanation," Aria said, pulling her phone out of her purse.

"Who are you calling?" Mo sniffled.

"Isa. You can't find Messiah, but wherever Isa is, Messiah will be. I'm going to have to throw this nigga some pussy after this, but no way is Messiah going to get away with this disappearing shit. We about to run down on his ass," Aria said.

Morgan laughed, through her tears, because Aria had been spoon-feeding Isa her time for months. Morgan desperately needed that laugh. It released a minuscule amount of sadness, but it was like taking a breath after your head had been immersed underwater. Good friends did that. Morgan had never had a genuine one, so she wasn't familiar with the load a good girl friend could help relieve.

Aria's fingers tapped on her iPhone screen and she snickered.

"This nigga better be careful with me. I'll mess around and give him a baby," Aria snickered.

Again, the dread on Morgan's heart eased, as she released a small smile and shook her head.

"Got it. They're at Bleu's. Let's go," Aria said.

Morgan was silent the entire drive. She didn't even bother to dress. She rode out in sweats and a ponytail, because she just wanted to lay eyes on him. She wanted him to lay eyes on her...to see the damage he had caused. Morgan's head rested against the passenger window, as the highway flashed in a blur outside. A part of her wished she had never loved him. A schoolgirl crush that he never acknowledged was much easier to get over. What they shared...the illusion of what she had assumed it to be... cut deeply. He had penetrated her very being and Morgan was struggling to accept that it was over. It had to be over. There was no other option...no other scenario in which the two of them could be together. Her family was her family, his family was his. They were at odds and would forever be. No love could exist there. Morgan questioned if anything he ever said to her was real. Had she just been a mark? A conquest to partake in just to spit on her dead father's legacy. Morgan was defeated. She had embarrassed her father's name. That pained her most. His name was all she had left of him. She hadn't been lucky like Raven. She had only experienced six years with him before he was taken. His name, wearing it proudly, having people recognize it with love, was all that remained. Messiah had made a fool of her.

They pulled up to Bleu's house and Morgan spotted the three BMW's sitting curbside. The sight of them pissed her off. Each of them had known. Messiah, Isa, and Ahmeek had all been privy to the deception. Had she been the butt of their jokes? Had this been one, long plot of disrespect? In an instant, her sadness transformed to irrational rage. She popped open the door to Aria's car, before Aria could even fully stop. Morgan was on a warpath, as she picked up one of the landscaping bricks that lined Bleu's pretty, manicured lawn. She tossed that shit through Messiah's front window. The alarm blared so loudly that her ears rang, but she didn't care. She bent down to grab another one, hoisting the large, heavy brick above her head.

"Ughh!" she screamed, as she chucked it toward car number two.

"Morgan!" Aria shouted, as she hopped out the car in shock, covering her mouth. Meek's windshield splintered. "Bitch, you have lost your whole mind!" Aria exclaimed. The car alarms blared, as Morgan went for Isa's. That nigga wasn't exempt from her wrath. He was Messiah's best friend. She had known him just as long as she'd known Messiah. *Fuck him too*, she thought, as she broke his window. Morgan went back to Messiah's car and removed her key, walking around it, scratching up the paint, as he emerged from the house.

"Yo, Mo! What the fuckkk?!" Meek uttered, in a calm discontent, as everyone came out onto the porch. He swiped a slow hand over his goatee, as they all looked at her in shock.

Morgan switched her pretty-ass around Messiah's car, scratching that shit up like she was drawing on a chalkboard. He stood there, watching her, hawking her, but not speaking, as she drew him a pretty picture on his $100,000-whip.

"Mo!" Bleu exclaimed, as she sauntered out of the house with sad eyes.

"Don't make it about you and it won't be about you, Bleu," Morgan said. She was in a different state of mind now that she had seen his face. This nigga. Her nigga. Her now ex-nigga. Had lied. Had disrespected. Then, he had the nerve to not answer his phone when she called him. Morgan was about to murder his ass.

"Yo! Nigga! That's custom paint," Isa protested, as he held up his hands. "This what you on, Ali?" That last question was for Aria.

Aria shrugged. "I might let you sniff it for your troubles," she said.

"Oh, I'ma do more than sniff that shit," Isa said. "I'ma put my tongue all in that shit, a couple times. Eating that ass too. You might as well get ready to put that shit on a plate."

Aria smirked. "Better be careful, boy, you might go crazy."

"You ain't got shit to say? You just gon' stand there? Like you didn't fuck up my whole life!" Morgan asked, tears coming to her, again. "Like your brother ain't the bitch-ass nigga that made me an orphan! Like you didn't have your tongue in my pussy, making me fall in love, while you were plotting on my whole family!"

"Yooo!" Meek said, wiping his hands down his waves, as his eyebrows lifted in stun. Dirty words on pretty Morgan's lips was too much for everybody.

She knew that last one would bring Messiah's ass off the porch. Somehow, he was still sensitive to his homeboys hearing about her sexual exploits.

He sauntered over to her, slowly, his jaw flexed, locked, in fact, so she knew he was pissed.

Good, motherfucka, me the fuck too.

He had definitely changed her. This moxie had been taught by him…it had come from him. He walked up on her, like a lion eyeing prey, causing her to backpedal until his car stopped her and then he trapped her, two arms on either side of her body, palms against the car as he leaned down over her.

"Go home, Mo," he said, in a low tone.

"Go home?" she asked, her tears finally falling as her lip quivered. "Go home?" she shrieked. "Messiah…" His name was a whisper on her lips, as if she was too ashamed to even be speaking it. His name. With the z's for s's. He closed his eyes and his nostrils flared, as he pressed his forehead to hers. He knew everyone was watching. This was the Morgan and Messiah show…the season finale…everyone was hanging on to every single second. Morgan closed her eyes, as she reached for his face.

"I trusted you," she cried. "You said it was real. In my room, on the floor, you said it was whatever I wanted it to be. I didn't want this. You said it was about me, but it wasn't. It was about revenge. Why would you do this to me? You wanted to hurt me. This entire time was about hurting me. How could you hurt me?"

"Messiah…" Bleu called.

He pulled back and Morgan crumbled. He pinched the bridge of his nose and took a step back. He turned his back on her and Morgan went after him. "You said it was real!" she shouted. It was like she was begging for acknowledgement. Begging him to verify the authenticity of what they shared.

"It was real!" he turned on her and shouted. "Okay? It was real, Mo! The fuck does that matter? Huh?" He was in her face, sneering angrily, in disgust, livid, confrontational.

"Messiah!" Bleu shouted, as she intervened, moving fast to get between Messiah and Morgan.

"Nah, Bleu! Let his fake-ass say what he got to say! Let him tell me more lies! Let him break my heart a little more because it ain't broke enough for him! I loved your broken-ass!"

"And I loved your broken-ass too!" he shouted over Bleu, who was pushing him back toward the porch.

"Yo, B! Quit fucking touching me! Ain't nobody gon' do nothing to her spoiled-ass!" Messiah barked. He focused back on Morgan. "You out here acting like a little-ass girl. Take yo' ass home!" Messiah pointed a stern finger toward Aria's car. Bleu stepped back, reluctantly, shooting worried eyes at Meek and Isa. Meek came down off the porch.

"No! I'm not going anywhere until you tell me the truth! You were going to hurt me? Huh? Was that the plan? Is that why everybody's so worried? They all standing around on eggshells like you gon' do something to me, Messiah. You were going to kill me? To get back at Ethic for killing Mizan?" She expected him to deny it immediately, but when he didn't, she scoffed, jerking her neck back in disbelief. She put a hand on her hip and one over her mouth, as she turned her back to him. She had to double over to stop the sickness in her stomach. Hands to knees, she squeezed her eyes shut. *He was.*

"Go home, Morgan," he said.

Morgan stood and turned to him, eyes flooded from the storm he had caused. "All this for Mizan," she whispered. She shook her head. "Your brother was a monster! He used to beat my sister's ass every day!"

"Fuck yo' sister, Mo! Same way you riding for yours, I'ma ride for mine!"

He was in her face, again, and Morgan swung, jabbing him across the chin.

Everybody came off the porch at that, but before they could stop him, Messiah had one strong hand wrapped around Morgan's fragile neck, holding her away at arm's length. Fire blazed in his eyes. He grit his teeth so hard it felt like they would chip, and his temple pulsed. Morgan stood there, hands at her sides, head slightly raised from the pressure of his hand, eyes pouring emotion. She lifted both her hands to the one that acted as a noose around her neck. She couldn't breathe, he was gripping her so tightly, but somehow, she knew it wasn't out of malice. He was holding on, not wanting to let go, because once he did, they were done. He was choking her and Morgan let him because without him she would die anyway. He released her, pushing her away from him like she disgusted him, and Aria pulled Mo back.

"Mo, let's just go," Aria whispered.

Morgan pulled away from Aria and pushed Messiah, hard, baiting him, inciting him. She was trying to trigger his aggression, trying to make him react, make him prove that he cared.

"Hurt me! Hurt me! Do it!" she shouted.

She swung and connected a second time.

Isa immediately stood off to the side, between Messiah and Morgan, in case Messiah lost his cool.

Messiah scoffed and shook his head, as he fingered his chin. She could throw a punch, that much was for sure. He tasted blood on his lip and he pulled it into his mouth, snickering. "You're on one side, I'm on the other. Ain't shit nobody can do about that."

Morgan wilted in front of him, gripping the front of her shirt in agony.

"And that's it? Just fuck me? You just leave without explaining this shit to me? You walk away like we never even happened? This meant something to me! It's that easy for you?"

"Easy as fuck, shorty. I don't need a motherfucker in this world. I came in this bitch dolo, I'ma die dolo. Go the fuck home! Forget you knew a nigga because I already forgot you."

Morgan recoiled like he had slapped her. His words cut her; shredded her little, spoiled-ass right up and blew her away in the wind. His perception was the saddest thing she had ever heard. How could he not need her? Not want her? How could she not live in the folds of his memory? In a compartment reserved for the type of love that changed your life? After the ways they had experienced one another, how could he just abandon the connection they had built? She needed every single piece of him, even these cruel parts, even the deceptive parts that were injuring her in this moment.

"Ssiah, no," she cried. She blubbered. Her tender heart was at his feet and he was dancing all over it, dirtying it up. She could barely stand she was so hurt. She wanted to use the leverage she had. She wanted to pull out that baby mama card she had tucked in her back pocket and use it against him because she knew it would make him stay, but Morgan didn't want him by force. She wanted him to choose her. She wanted him to want her the way that she wanted him...to need her the way she needed him. Obligation was forced. She didn't want that. "You're loving me wrong. You told me to tell you and I'm telling you. I'm begging you. Please, Messiah. You're the only person who ever really heard me and now you're fucking everything up. You're loving me all wrong. Baby, please." Morgan gripped her shirt and pulled at the fabric, with every word, as if she could rip her own heart out.

"That should let you know I don't give a fuck no more, Mo," Messiah said.

"That's enough, bro," Meek said, finally speaking. The look on his face, as well as everyone else witnessing the dispute, was somber. Heartbreak was contagious.

Mo nodded, as if a sudden revelation came to her, as if she was seeing him for the first time. She was destroyed. Hurricane Messiah had leveled her. He had done irreparable damage. Morgan slid the diamond ring off her finger and tossed it at his chest.

"Fuck it," she whispered. "I give up. I'm done." Hindsight was 20/20 and she regretted ever believing that he could treat her any different than he treated the rest of the world. She allowed Aria to lead her to the car, but Isa halted them.

"Nah, Ali," he called out, as he sauntered over to the car. His light skin was covered in tattoos. Dark ink camouflaged both arms, all the way up the back of his neck and over his right eye, right against his hairline was a gun. He leaned his tall frame into the driver's side window. "Yo, I'm tryna taste that," he whispered, as he sipped from a Styrofoam cup.

"Where yo' mama at, boy? Because if she don't beat your ass, I'm going to! Who taught you how to talk to women? Does all this work for you?" she asked, as she motioned her hand up and down. "The unlimited Gucci drip, licking of lips, and crass talk, and shit?"

"Nah, ain't nobody checking for the god," he smirked, as he looked off down the block, while running both hands over his head. She knew it was a lie. He was a hood nigga, a local trap star, wrapped up in nothing but finesse, designer labels, and ink. She would bet her life on it that he had the type of dick that made girls lose their minds. She hadn't fallen victim to it, refusing to be another notch on his belt; but if this nigga kept looking for trouble, she was going to make him put his face in it. Like a bad dog that you trained when he shitted on your carpet. Aria wanted to rub his face all in it… make a whole mess out of his fine-ass. She shook her head. "Don't you see my friend over here hurting because of your homeboy? Do you really think I'm interested in what that mouth do, right now?" Aria snapped.

"Aria, just drive," Morgan whispered. "Isa, just let us leave." Her voice was so depleted. She lacked everything…love, confidence, energy, fight, but most of all, she was lacking Messiah. He was no longer hers and Morgan was dying…a slow…painful…death. Morgan was two seconds from losing it. She could feel the anxiety building in her.

Isa nodded, getting serious for a moment, as the severity of the situation distracted him from Aria.

"You had to do a nigga car like that, huh, Mo?" Isa asked.

"You knew, so fuck you too," Mo answered, without looking at him.

"Yo, Morgan. He was never going to touch you. That was never the move, if that makes it any better."

"It doesn't," Mo said it so low, he barely heard her, and she gazed out the window, as she watched Messiah disappear inside the house. "Aria, drive, damn!"

Aria put the car in gear. "Bye, rude-ass," she dismissed, as she rolled away from the curb.

Morgan was grateful that she could hold in her destruction until they started moving. Her cries folded her in half and she leaned over in her lap. The motion of the car killed her because she was driving away, putting distance between her and Messiah, and she knew it was officially over.

CHAPTER 12

I t's been a rough week for us," Alani said. She sat next to Ethic, her hands tucked in between her thighs, as she flexed up onto her tip toes. Her leg bounced. She was nervous. She couldn't control the energy, as that leg went to work against the wooden floor, her high heel setting a cadence for the room.

Tap, tap, tap, tap.

Ethic placed one hand to her knee, and like magic, she calmed. He leaned into her to whisper in her ear. "Relax."

It was a command. She followed.

Nyair sat on the other side of the desk, dressed down as usual. LeBron Lakers jersey over jeans, and Jordan's on his feet. He finessed the hair on his chin, as he took them in.

"What's the deal, bruh? Was it a rough week or was it a week of Alani overthinking, overanalyzing?" Nyair said.

Alani frowned and rolled her eyes. "So, what y'all go out for one drink and now it's gang gang against little ol' me in these sessions?" she asked, snickering.

"Women and men's perceptions differ. What's a mountain for you might be a molehill for Ethic," Nyair said.

"It's been a rough week," Ethic confirmed. Alani stuck out her tongue and rolled her eyes, eliciting a smirk from Nyair. Ethic didn't miss their chemistry. Alani was lighthearted with Nyair, childish even, like they had years and years of inside jokes that kept them bonded.

"How so?" Nyair asked.

"A friend turned out to be foe," Ethic said, vaguely, as he leaned onto his knees and rubbed the back of his neck, like this conversation took so much, like he had somewhere else to be. His heart wasn't in this session. He was worried about so many things. About Mo, about Messiah coming back, about Raven, about how he hadn't been able to foresee this treachery.

"And you wanted to punish him for that," Nyair said. "She didn't want you to. Now, it's eating away at you because a man that let's disrespect slide ain't a man?"

Ethic rolled stern eyes up to Nyair. They froze on him, but Nyair didn't look down. Church boy had no bitch in him. Ethic was impressed. He had set across from plenty men who claimed to be tough that couldn't look him in the eyes. He smirked. Nyair continued.

"That's the code you're used to living by, right? Betrayal is punishable by what? Death? Torture? Speak frankly, my man. This is personal counsel, nothing leaves this room."

Ethic's nostrils flared, and his jaw locked, as he laced his hands. He punched his right hand into his left palm, slightly, weighing on Nyair's question. No way would he ever answer aloud, but in his mind, an effortless *death*, rang out.

"Silence is loud, G. Sometimes, it's in what you don't say," Nyair said.

"G, this? G, that? I'm having a hard time reconciling that," Ethic said. Alani marked Ethic with astonished eyes. He was in a mood, had been in a mood, all week. She had never seen him this way...short with people, irritated with redundancy, even his tone with the kids was different. He was never mean, but his patience had diminished, like deep thoughts occupied every space of his mind and they were constantly interrupting. Sex was darker, deeper, harder...motherfucking good, but his touch had changed like the hues of a mood ring. Messiah's betrayal haunted him...another ghost for her king to carry, only this one still lived and breathed, and she knew that was the thing that bothered him most. Ethic was in the mood for murder.

"G for me stands for God, Ethic. Black men all over the world have forgotten the God in them. Kings brought over here on slave ships, surviving that, watching our women raped, our babies ripped from the nipples of their mothers, emasculated. I'm here to remind you that you're a god. Black, strong, resilient. So, when I say that, I mean *my G*. My god. Because you're made of His making, of his image. You aren't of this walk of life, so you don't know yet...the power you have. You know the power the streets show you, but that's man-made. I'm talking about power you were born with that you haven't even accessed yet. Forgiveness is one of those powers. It's how Alani's able to sit next to you right now."

"Some shit is…" he paused, remembering where he was, and he cleared his throat. "Some things are unforgivable."

"But only when it offends you, right?" Alani's voice was tiny and full of injury. "Or is it about Raven? When it pertains to Raven, it's unforgivable? But when it's about my hurt, that should be forgiven?"

Ethic felt the temperature rise in the room. He had fucked up. He had placed expectations on her that he couldn't meet himself. A double standard, he knew it, but shit shook out that way sometimes. Over Raven, it shook out that way every time.

"That's not what I'm saying," he said. "I'm here with you. I'm trying to be a better man for you. That old way is still in me, fighting that…feels like pulling teeth. It doesn't just go away overnight."

"And it won't. Change is slow. Fast change is an illusion. Whomever this friend is, he's worth your forgiveness. I know that simply because you're hurt by this. Betrayal from a stranger, from somebody you don't love, doesn't affect you. You loved him, and to love a person, you have to know that they will hurt you one day because we're human. We're imperfect. So, hurt is a part of the equation. That's what forgiveness is for. To keep the people you love in your life after they've damaged you. Forgiveness is for you, not them."

Ethic sat back in his chair, in deep contemplation.

"There's discord between the two of you. Tension that this situation brings up that affects the two of you. You've been exchanging the tension back and forth, trying to exhaust it out of you, through sex, passing demons, back and forth. It's time to refrain. It's time to cleanse and connect spiritually. The dating...y'all started that yet?"

"So much has happened. We haven't had time," Alani said.

"Make time," Nyair said.

Ethic lifted from his chair, impatient, irritated, suffocating in this church where he was thinking of the worst. He just needed some air.

He shook Nyair's hand.

"Good seeing you, G," Nyair said.

Ethic placed his hand on the small of Alani's back, as she stood, and led her out of the office. They didn't speak. Ethic didn't like this feeling. This disdain he felt from her, like her resentment was resurfacing, because of what he'd said. He followed her to the car, both hands tucked in his Armani slacks and his eyes toward the ground, as his thoughts ambushed him.

He walked her to the passenger side and when she reached for the door he pushed it closed and forced her against it.

"I'm sorry for my energy this past week, for brooding, for making it uncomfortable for you," he said.

"Tell me about Raven," she whispered. "About what happened to her. About what she meant to you. About what I mean to you. It kind of feels like I'm a consolation prize..."

"You're not," he said. She looked off to the side. He put gentle fingers to her chin, steering her back, before she got lost in her thoughts...before she amplified their problems in her heart. "You're not," he repeated. "I just can't talk about that. One day, but not today, and I need you to understand that."

Alani didn't speak, her brows were dipped, her body language stiff. He nodded. She was on her stubborn shit. Her Alani shit. He opened her door, and when she was inside, he closed it, and then made his way to the driver's seat. Silence filled their car ride and when she saw him merging onto the highway to head back to his home, she said, "Take me home, please."

His brows lifted in stun, but he didn't argue with her. He changed course, headed to her house. Perhaps, a night apart to clear the air and get his mind right would do them both well.

"I want to take you somewhere," he said. "For the weekend. Pack a bag. I'll pick you up tomorrow."

"You sure this is the best time to go away overnight? The kids..."

"Will stay with Lily. I'll have Mo come home for the weekend."

"Morgan just went through so much. It feels like you should be home, in case she needs you," Alani said. "And Lily has a family, Ethic..."

"So, you don't want to go? Just say that, because all the rest just sounds like excuses. You said slow. If this is fast, I can fall back." Ethic stated.

"If that's what you want to do," Alani said.

Ethic shook his head. *Stubborn-ass.* Alani could be so damned difficult at times. She was work. She was the hardest work he had ever done.

She rolled her eyes. "Call Morgan and make sure she's fine with you leaving town for a few days and then bring the kids here. Nannie would love the company and I'll feel better about leaving her."

Ethic nodded. "Fine," he said.

"Fine," she shot back.

"Hey." One word jarred her attention. "You keep acting like you need to be fucked and that celibacy shit we just promised Nyair is getting tossed right out the fucking window." Ethic licked his lips, like remnants of her pussy lingered there, and Alani blushed so hard that even her fingertips heated and then turned red.

He pushed open the door and rounded the car to open hers. She stood and attempted to walk pass him. He caught her hand and pulled her back. A hand to the small of her back and one gripping her chin, he kissed her. Alani didn't want to like it, but damn if she didn't love that shit.

He released her, and she gave up a stubborn smile.

"Friday, Ms. Hill," he said.

She nodded, and he watched her waltz up the walkway. "That attitude should be gone by then," he shouted after her. Alani turned to him, lifting an eyebrow in defiance, then walked into her house. Not until she was safely inside did he get into his Range and drive away.

CHAPTER 13

Ethic placed hard-bottomed Gucci loafers to the tile floor, as he stepped into the hospital. The place had a peculiar smell. He had lived in it for weeks when he was trapped between these walls, after being shot. It reeked of death…of Love's death…of Raven's…that was the problem with small towns. It only had one of everything. One hospital. One jail. One courthouse. The memories… all the deaths he had collected along the years had occurred under this very roof. It put him in a foul mood. Ghosts clung to the corridors of this building. Ethic could feel them. He had come too close to being one of the souls lost here, so he knew they dwelled sight unseen, but felt - if one took the time to still long enough to acknowledge the energy. It came with a chill down one's spine or the raised hair on the back of one's neck. Even the feeling of company occupying a space that appeared desolate. In this hospital, those feelings came with company…the presence of lives lost…when medicine failed…Ethic wanted to get out of there as quick as possible, but he had to see one man first.

Ethic passed the nurses' station and recognized the nurse he had paid to look after Nannie. No words were needed for her to lift out her seat. He walked by her, without acknowledgement. The sound of the fire alarm erupted moments later and Ethic watched as the nurse rushed to the armed guard standing in front of one of the rooms.

"Everyone must clear the floor," she said. "I'm sorry. He's handcuffed to the bed. All patients will be looked after by staff, but when that alarm goes off, the floor must clear."

She ushered the guard to the elevator and then walked away. Ethic waited until the elevator doors closed before taking a casual stroll down the hall and sliding inside the room.

The dimmed lights cast a shadow over the room and a body lie beneath white sheets on the hospital bed.

"Who's there?"

Ethic stepped out of the darkness that concealed him and stood next to the bed.

"A nigga you been trying to see, apparently," Ethic replied, as he stared into the eyes of Bookie Grant, Messiah's father, Benny Atkins' adversary.

Bookie's eyes doubled in size, as Ethic stood over him.

"You sent Messiah for me. After I fucking murdered your first son, you sent your second son to my doorstep, knowing that I would murder him too. What type of man sends his son to do his dirty work?" Ethic asked.

"Fuck you, motherfucker," Bookie sneered.

Ethic scoffed. "That's what you do, right? Fuck men. Molest boys? Messiah?" Ethic asked, darkness dancing in his eyes at the thought of how many young boys he had taken advantage of over the years, before being locked up. "That's why he did it, right?" Ethic asked. "Because you stripped your son of his manhood when he was a kid. He's terrified of you and you used that against him. Niggas like you," Ethic stated, in disgust, shaking his head. He clicked a button on the beeping heart monitor beside the bed and the green lights on the interface turned off. "You like molesting little boys...your son...your own flesh and blood..."

Bookie shook, uncontrollably, as Ethic spilled his darkest secrets. "That boy's a fucking liar..."

Ethic slipped a leather glove over his hand and covered Bookie's mouth and nose with it before Bookie could finish his sentence. He pressed so hard that Bookie couldn't breathe.

"That boy's my fucking brother," Ethic sneered. He kicked and bucked in the bed, as Ethic stared him in the eyes, with an expression so calm that it seemed demonic. "You should have left well enough alone," Ethic said. "Any nigga that ever sent for me got shipped back in a body bag. You knew better."

Bookie's eyes bulged out of his head, as Ethic watched the blood vessels burst one by one, making the whites of his eyes streak with red. Bookie was cuffed to the railing of the bed and it clanged violently, as he struggled. He reached for Ethic's hand with his one free hand, but Ethic's hand was pressed so tightly against his airway that Bookie couldn't steal one sip of oxygen.

"Feel every second," Ethic whispered. Ethic felt the strength leaving Bookie's body and he felt no remorse. He was a man who didn't enjoy murder. He committed it when necessary...only when provoked, but this one...he reveled in...he indulged in it...until every, single sign of life was gone. He removed the glove and put it in his pocket and then walked back into the hallway, blending in with the hustle and bustle of the staff. Ethic bypassed the nurse and slid an envelope stuffed with hundred-dollar bills into the front pocket of her scrubs, never stopping his stride, as he headed for the stairway. She would "discover" the body and remove the pieces of tape she had placed over the cameras that recorded movement on the wing where Bookie had occupied. It was a flawlessly executed kill, and as Ethic walked out of the hospital, he hoped it would be his last.

CHAPTER 14

Ethic rolled his Range Rover to a stop in front of Alani's house. He stalled, as he placed the car in park. Anxiety filled him. He was nervous. It was a foreign feeling. The hollow pit in the bottom of his stomach. The sweaty palms. He had never felt this way before. It wasn't until this very moment that he realized he had never taken a woman on a real date. The streets hadn't left him much time for courtship. He had enjoyed time with women. Hotel rooms and sex, breakfast afterward, but he had never engaged in wooing a woman. It wasn't required. Women were taken with him at hello and not because he tried, but because he was just a force…a presence…a marvel of a man that made women want to experience him between their legs. He filled their hearts effortlessly with his authenticity, but only a particular few had the power to occupy his in return. No one had ever held that expectation of him. Dating. Women never required that of him. It was hello and then orgasms. Nothing in between. Alani's pre-requisite was different. It was a challenge and it brought out the young man in him. He glanced over at the bouquet of long stem lilies. A phone call to Nannie had given him the leg up on Alani's favorite flower. It felt corny, showing up with flowers, especially from a local boutique. They were average, at best, not like the La Fleur roses he had given her before, but he had taken the time to stop at a local florist to pick each one himself. The florist had taught him how to arrange the bouquet, personally, because if he was going to gift them, he wanted each petal to have meaning…to be selected by him for her.

"Are we going in?" Eazy asked, impatiently.

Ethic looked up at the house and took a deep breath. Fucking nerves, he thought, feeling juvenile.

"Yeah, Big Man, let's go," Ethic said, as he stepped out the car and opened the back door for his children. They spilled out and Eazy bolted for the porch, while Bella strolled to her own pace, as ear buds drowned out the world around her. Nannie came spilling out the front door, as if she had been waiting for their arrival.

"My babies," she greeted.

"Hi, Nannie!" Eazy shouted, as he ran into her, wrapping her in a rough hug. Ethic paused at the bottom of the steps when he heard Eazy use the term of endearment. Only Alani called her Nannie. She pronounced it like Nay-nee, because she hadn't been able to say auntie as a baby, and it had just stuck; but no one else called the old woman that. Everyone else called her Pat. Ethic called her Beautiful. To his children, she was their 'Nannie' as well, because the old woman smiled as she embraced them.

"Careful, Eazy," Ethic said, as he climbed the steps and leaned down to kiss the old woman's cheek. He handed her a bouquet of African Daisies; the same flowers he had filled her hospital room with, day in and day out.

"Thank you, Ezra," Nannie said, as she patted his cheek.

Ethic turned to his children. "Do I need to tell y'all to behave? I know I don't because y'all know better, right?"

"Boy, hush," Nannie said. "Kids will be kids. If they're too quiet and boring, I might as well be hanging with old folks. I need their energy around here. We're going to have us a good ol' time. Ain't that right?" She looked to Bella and tapped the tip of her nose.

Bella beamed.

"Get on in the house and don't put y'all dirty shoes on my new carpet. Take them shoes off at the door," Nannie fussed.

Ethic's heart warmed. It all felt like family. The chastising, the elderly figure spoiling his children, ignoring his rules and making up her own because she was the boss. He loved this shit. He would do anything to preserve these bonds his children were making. They deserved them, and he yearned for them.

"Is she ready?" he asked.

"She damn well should be. She's been getting ready all morning," Nannie fussed. "Come on in, baby."

Ethic hesitated, and Nannie's brow crinkled, as she watched him halt at the threshold like someone had put a hex on his feet.

"You're welcome here, Ezra. Get on in here, now," she said.

Ethic's heart lurched, as he stepped inside. He had such

bad memories between these walls. He had committed the ultimate sin here, and being here was like holding up a mirror to see the monster that he kept dormant inside. His kids' shoes were strewn about by the front door and they were heading to the living room.

"Yo!" he called to them. They turned. He pointed to their mess and they backtracked, instantly, lining the shoes up neatly. "Thank you. Daddy can't get no love before I leave?"

They gave him quick hugs and then rushed off with Nannie to the living room.

Ethic stood by the front door, not daring enough to venture further, as he waited. Butterflies filled him, and he paced slightly, until he heard, "Hey."

He turned and looked up to find Alani standing there. "You're a fucking vision, baby," he said. Alani blushed and smiled so wide that he had to put a hand over the left side of his chest. She was shooting invisible arrows at him. He felt each one, as she descended the stairs.

"It's just jeans, Ethic," she said, with a blush, as she rolled her eyes, bashful from his appreciation. She looked down at the dark denim, skin-tight pants and slightly lighter toned denim button-down shirt. "You said casual," she said.

"Casual looks fucking amazing on you," he complimented, as he pulled her hand, whipping her body into him and putting a hand behind her neck. He stood there, silent, eyes taking her in, every inch of her face as she gazed up at him. Words weren't needed. She knew what he was doing...taking his time...to store her image in his memory. Appreciating, he called it. Long extensions fell down her back in bouncy curls and Ethic's hands moved up, playing with the baby hair that rested at the nape of her neck.

"Don't you put your hands in my hair, boy," she warned. "It took hours for me to look this good."

He chuckled and nodded. That was black girl shit... black girl rules...black girl talk. He respected it and lowered his hands. He handed her the flowers and then studied her reaction, as a genuine smile spread east to west on her face. She closed her eyes and brought the bouquet to her nose, before taking a deep breath. She liked them. He could tell by the way the wrinkles in the center of her forehead disappeared and she sighed to release the fragrance from the breath she held for an extra beat. She was simple to please. He liked that. It meant she could ride through a drought with him - if he ever needed her to...she would never see that day, because if Ethic knew nothing else, he knew how to make money, but it was good to know she wasn't materialistic. It was the nuances he would pick up while dating her, the little things. Maybe she was on to something.

"Thank you," she said.

"You ready to get out of here?"

She nodded. "Just let me put these in some water and see the kids first."

The kids, he thought. It stuck out every time she said it. Not his kids, but *the* kids. He was trusting her more and more to be a part of their lives. The more she said it, the more he felt like she just may be around to stay this time, because... well, she had the kids to think about. It warmed him every time. She frowned, as she slipped into her jacket.

"What?" she asked, as he stared at her with a pinched brow. He was so introspective, so brooding. He shook his head. He had to remember not to show how amazed he was by her.

"Nothing," he replied, as he took slow steps behind her toward the living room.

"So, y'all just not going to show me no love?" Alani asked, when she spotted them.

"Sorry, Alani," Bella called from the rocking chair, as she sat with lotto slips in front of her, filling in random numbers. Nannie had her predicting the lottery numbers and Alani smiled because she used to love to do that when she was a child. Eazy ran into Alani, hugging her.

"Hey, Big Man," she greeted.

"Can I come on the date?" Eazy asked.

Alani shook her head. "Not this time, but I promise you and I will have our own day to spend together one day this week. I'll surprise you, one day after school. That sound legit?" she asked.

"What about me?" Bella asked.

"We already have Saturdays, B," Alani responded. "This one is just for me and Eazy. You can do me a favor and put these in water, though." She extended the flowers and Bella rose from her seat to retrieve them. "We'll see y'all Sunday, okay?"

Ethic watched Alani command his children, as if she had been around them their entire lives. They didn't resist her. They didn't back talk; and if they did, she shut them down

ASHLEY ANTOINETTE

with love, not malice. She was stern yet loving, kind and unbelievably patient. Dolce had been around them forever and didn't have the shorthand that Alani showed with them. Eazy returned to Nannie's side and the couple turned to leave.

"Love you, Daddy. Love you, Alani," Bella called.

Ethic felt tension fill his chest. That was pressure. He didn't want that for Alani. The push to respond just because his child had put her on the spot, but an effortless, "I love you more," fell from Alani's lips, as she snatched up her purse. Ethic wanted to fuck her. It was shit like that...it made dating seem trivial. Ethic needed to marry this woman. He wanted to carry her upstairs and root himself so deeply in her that separating them would be impossible. He wanted to create family with her, legacy...he wanted to hear her scream his name first, while he beat it, then while she birthed the result of the seed he would plant.

"Love you, baby girl," Ethic added, then he took Alani's hand and led her to his car. He opened the passenger door for her and she slid into the seat. She turned to put on her seat belt, and when she turned back, Ethic was there, taking her tongue into his mouth. She melted into him, moaning, slightly, as he awakened her body.

"You taste so fucking good," he whispered. "How am I supposed to not touch you? Nyair on that bullshit."

Alani laughed, as she placed a hand on his cheek. "Kisses are fine," she whispered. "He said no sex."

Ethic bit his bottom lip like it would be impossible and

169

Alani felt herself turn red. "No sex," he confirmed, with a head nod. "Okay, no sex." He closed her door and then rounded the back of the car, before joining her inside.

Ethic placed his hand on her thigh, one hand gripping the steering wheel, and he pulled off. That one hand made her feel so secure, like there wasn't another person in the world that could get to her, as long as it was placed there. Ethic was a man that provided reassurance. As long as the two of them were right, everything else around them could be all wrong and Alani wouldn't feel it.

"So, where are we going?" she asked.

"Somewhere beautiful. The scenery has to match my company," he said.

"Hmm," she replied, as if she was figuring something out all of a sudden.

"What?" he countered.

"That explains why you took that other bitch to a diner," she said, with the roll of her eyes.

Ethic snickered. "You're ruthless," he stated with, a shake of his head.

"Over you, I absolutely am," she admitted. She rolled jealous eyes out the window. She hated that she had even brought her up. "It killed me, seeing you with her. Seeing you with green eyes too. Like it gutted me, Ethic."

Ethic kept his eyes on the road, but he responded, "Sometimes, you find a spot that's exquisite. The sun shines on it just right, and you just don't want to see anything more. You're fine, right there in that spot. You're satisfied, and you forget about all the other shit you've seen before." His grip on her thigh tightened and Alani sighed, in relief, as she looked out her window.

They drove for so long that Alani drifted to sleep. When she felt the car stop, she lifted her head and rubbed her sore neck.

"Where are we?" she asked, as she looked outside her window, in wonder. A beautiful, large, white house with wide shutters, and a wraparound porch sat in the distance. Fields surrounded it and a large, red barn sat on the property. Creaking from the porch swing whined through the air, as the sound of water washing ashore added harmony.

"You wanted me to date you. This is our first date," he said.

"Second," she corrected. "I made you dinner, remember?"

"Nah, that don't count. We washing that. Our time begins here. It's important. The starting over and such."

She took pause to meet his earnest gaze and she nodded. Ethic climbed out the car and she waited for him to open her door. He pulled it open and then reached into the backseat for her bag. He took her hand and Alani felt it. The connection. The passion burning from his fingertips to hers. He loved her so much; so much that he made her feel like wrong was right. She followed him to the house and when they climbed up the porch's stairs, she reached for the handle on the door. She pressed down and then pushed.

"It's locked," she said, frowning. "Is someone expecting us?" Ethic came up behind her and went into his pocket, producing a key. He opened the door.

"You have a key?"

"I should. I own it," he said.

"You own this farm?" she asked, confused. He nodded and pushed inside the home, leaving Alani standing, perplexed, on the front porch. She eased through the door to the stuffy home. Stale air lingered inside, as if the door hadn't been opened for months. She looked at him, stunned.

"What?" Ethic asked.

Alani smiled, while shaking her head. He was the opposite of what every woman would assume him to be. He was cultured and worldly and unique. With him, she would have to expect the unexpected because everything she assumed of him was wrong. "It's really beautiful. I just didn't expect you to own a farm. Are there animals?" she asked.

He nodded. "I don't run it. I pay a nice, old woman and her husband to tend to it. I just believe in owning land. You never know when you'll have to live off the land. The world is crazy. Politics, war, racism. Cops killing black boys every day with no retribution. One day, I might have to retreat here. I want my family to always have a place to come that's removed from it all, if it ever comes to that," he said. "And, yeah, there's animals. I want to show you something."

Alani followed him through the kitchen and out the back door, as they headed toward a huge, wooden barn in the back. Alani tiptoed over mud puddles and dirt.

"Ethic, my shoes. I just bought them," she said, hating to sound like that girl, but she had spent a grip on the red-soled bottoms to try to match his fly and she'd be damned if she got mud all over them.

He turned, in surprise, and then eyed the shoes on her feet. They didn't even look like something she'd wear. He knew her well enough to realize she had put effort into trying to impress him. This date meant something to her. The shoes, the hair. Her comments about Dolce and YaYa. Nannie's complaints about the time it had taken Alani to prepare. Alani had tried to be what she assumed he liked. She had tried to be like them. Bad bitches, she had called them once. It broke his heart that she felt the need to even compete, but he didn't want to embarrass her. She had always come off so strong and self-assured. He saw holes in her, ones he hadn't put there that he would need to fill.

"Can't have that," he said, with a wink. "Hop on my back."

She shook her head, smiling, as she grabbed his shoulders and jumped up. She wrapped her arms around his neck tightly, as he bounced her higher, then she put her lips near his ear, biting it softly. When he carried her into the wooden structure, Alani looked around, in wonder.

"Ethic, you have horses?" she asked, as she hopped down, instantly, forgetting all about the shoes. She covered her mouth with both hands to contain her excitement. Her eyes were wide like a child seeing an elephant for the first time at the circus. "You own fucking horses?"

"One for every person I love," he said. Alani counted the horses.

"There's six horses," she said.

"One for each of my kids, one for Eazy's mom, and one for..."

"Me?" she asked. She didn't miss how he included Love. He always included their dead son. He always included her. Her eyes watered. He nodded, as he opened the stall. Inside, was a white Mustang, standing tall and strong.

"You bought me a horse?" she asked.

"She doesn't have a name yet," Ethic said, as Alani crept inside. The horse huffed, and Alani jumped.

"She's not used to people. I buy them wild. I pay a wrangler to train them, domesticate them. She's a stubborn girl. She hasn't allowed anyone to touch her. Horses are empathetic creatures. They're therapeutic, but it takes the right person to connect with them."

Ethic went to touch the Mustang and she bucked, lifting on hind legs. Alani jumped back.

Alani inched forward, reaching out with trembling fingers. The horse huffed and tried to back up, but the stall she was berthed in stopped her.

"I don't know anything about horses," she whispered, her voice catching on fear because she expected this creature to buck at her any moment.

"That horse doesn't know anything about you either," Ethic said, in a low tone, as he leaned back, crossing his arms across his broad chest as he witnessed the interaction. "I think you're on fair ground."

Alani couldn't tear her eyes off the animal, as she took a step closer, until just her fingertips rested on its muzzle. She pulled back as the horse reacted, neighing and backing up. The horse was panicking, and Alani was too. Her heart was beating so rapidly it felt like it would jump out of her chest.

"She feels trapped. She's sad. Look at her eyes, Ethic," Alani whispered. She knew what that felt like and the wetness that shone in the huge, auburn eyes of this beast couldn't be anything other than emotion.

"I'm sure she is. She lost her foal," Ethic informed.

"Foal?" Alani asked, as she turned to meet Ethic's gaze.

"She was pregnant. The foal didn't make it," he said.

Alani's eyes snapped back to the horse, her horse, and her stomach plummeted. It suddenly felt like she was looking into a mirror. "It's okay," she whispered. She rested her palm on its muzzle and brought her other hand to the horse's neck. "It's okay." The horse huffed, again and again, as Alani rubbed. "I know."

She scoffed, in disbelief. She knew that feeling. She had lost her foal too, to foul play, and it was unfair and devastating, and crushing, and it hurt so fucking bad that Alani's eyes watered. "You are beautiful," she said, as she rubbed its coat. The horse calmed at her touch. Alani felt her heart calm too.

"She likes you," Ethic said.

"Wow," Alani whispered, breathlessly.

Alani's heart swelled, as she stepped closer, resting her head on the side of the horse's long neck, and rubbing gently. "I can hear her heart beating," Alani whispered. "It's incredible. She's strong. She's heartbroken, but she's strong." Alani's eyes closed. "She's going to be just fine, now that she has someone to love it away." Alani wasn't speaking about the horse anymore and Ethic stood back, watching. A lovely fucking sight.

"She needs a name," Ethic said.

Alani turned to him. "Is she really mine?"

Ethic nodded. "She's really yours."

"Kenzie," she said, without hesitation. "Her name is Kenzie."

Ethic nodded. He had known that would be the name she would choose, before it even fell off her lips.

"Can I ride her?" Alani asked.

"Not yet," Ethic said. "There are others here you can ride. She would throw you. You've got to let the trainers tame her first. She wouldn't even let you put a saddle on her right now. She's used to being wild."

"She doesn't trust anyone enough to be tied down," Alani whispered. "She's afraid she'll end up hurt."

Alani looked to him and he nodded. Her chest rocked, and a sob escaped her lips.

"Nobody's going to hurt her here. I know she's been hurt before, but it won't happen ever again," Ethic said. His stare penetrated her, and Alani rushed into his arms. Fuck her hair. He fisted it, as he pressed her into his chest, while she cried. "I promise." Ethic knew she came with baggage. Some he had put on her, some other men before him had left her with. He would help unpack it all because she was home. She'd never need to carry it around again. Through every storm, his roof would cover her. His walls would protect her. She pulled back and lifted her lips to his. Their kiss was deep, desperate, sloppy. He placed his hands under her ass and scooped her, as her legs wrapped around his waist.

"I don't know if you'll call me after today," she whispered, between kisses.

"What?" Ethic pulled back, in confusion, trying to assess her meaning. He frowned, contemplating hard, as she panted in lust.

"I'm a whole ho out here because I'm fucking on the first date," she whispered, before reaching her hand down, massaging his erection through the fabric of his jeans.

"Is that right?" he asked.

She nodded. "Sucking dick and all."

CHAPTER 15

Ethic carried her in his arms, as he took heavy steps back toward the house. She commanded his focus, devouring his tongue, as he held her securely, hands on her ass. He groaned because her kisses did something to him, they set him on fire, and put a need in him that only she could fill…needs that they had been restricted from satisfying because they were on a quest to connect spiritually. His spirit was telling him to fuck her. The way she was whimpering, just from the taste of his thick tongue, told him her spirit was saying the same. The yard was full of mud from yesterday's rain and Ethic needed his eyes. He needed to detach his lips from hers, so he could navigate through the mess. He was dying to get her back to the house, to a bed, because his dick was already making plans. The taste of her tongue made him crave another piece of her flesh. His favorite set of lips. He missed them. He was starved for them, but Alani was too aggressive. She was all over him, practically climbing his frame to try to keep her pussy glued to the friction of his hardness. Ethic lost his balance.

"Oh shit!" he uttered, in alarm, as he held tight to her waist, turning his back so he landed on the bottom and she landed on top. Mud covered them, as Alani laughed…hollered…

screamed in amusement. It had been a long time since she had laughed so hard. It came from her gut, so heavily that it hurt...it hurt so good. Ethic shook his head. A low rumble echoed in his belly, laughing too. Alani picked up a glob of mud and smacked it against his cheek, before kissing him again. He nodded and winced, as she spread those dirty fingers all in his beard.

"Nice," he grumbled.

"Nothing's wrong with a little bit of mud," she snickered. "I like it a little dirty."

Ethic flipped her.

"Agh! My weave!"

Ethic took her chin in between the 'U' of one hand and pierced her with his stare. "Fuck the hair. Fuck the shoes. Fuck everything you think you need to keep my attention. You got it. You got me. I ain't the catch, baby. You are. Let me work to keep you, not the other way around. Okay?"

She nodded, then...

SPLAT!

A face full of mud.

"I'ma fuck you up," he snickered. She scrambled to her feet, laughing her ass off. She took off running. He gave chase, catching her with ease, and putting her over his shoulder. She went kicking and screaming, in laughter, as he carried her into the house. He placed her on her feet and the smile on her face was brilliant. The one on his felt foreign. It had been a long time since he had been this at ease. His children were safe, and he had a woman who loved him. He had never had both things simultaneously and it felt amazing. He was a simple man to please. Those two things were all he required.

"I'm sorry," she laughed. Ethic swiped mud from his face, even digging some out of his ear, as he grimaced. He removed his shirt. The sight of chocolate and abs made her throat constrict. She swallowed down lust. Then, he stepped out of his jeans. Then peeled off his socks. Then his drawers. He stood before her, the arrogant smirk on his face told her he wasn't shy as he covered his manhood, unable to hide it because something so massive couldn't be concealed with one hand. She undressed and stood there as his eyes took her in. She didn't cover anything. For the first time ever in her life, she felt beautiful in her skin. If Ethic liked it, it had to be enough because he was the prototype of a perfect man; and if a bitch disagreed, fuck her, because Ethic was perfect to Alani.

"Ny said no sex," Ethic stated.

"Okay," she said, with a shoulder shrug, as she walked over to him. "Let's see how long you keep singing that same tune. I'm walking around this house, all day, naked, until I get what I want."

"I'll enjoy the visual," Ethic chuckled. "But you ain't getting no dick."

Alani wrapped her arms around his neck and kissed his chest, and then ran a flat tongue up the center of his neck. She felt his manhood react.

"Let's get you cleaned up," he said, voice throaty, needy, as he tapped her ass.

He led the way out of the kitchen and up the stairs of the country house, grabbing their bags along the way.

Alani grew distracted at the opulence of the remodeled home. It was magnificent. Every room she passed was perfectly designed, and when they reached the bathroom, she swooned. It was the size of her living room.

"Tub or shower?" he asked.

"I've showered with you before. I want to bathe," she answered, sweetly. She dug in her scalp. "Do you have scissors?"

He pulled open a drawer near the sink and handed them over, then went to fill the tub. Alani stood in front of the mirror, cutting away at the extensions, as Ethic submerged inside the large jacuzzi tub.

"Come here," he said.

"Give me a minute. I just need to get this out. There's mud everywhere," she groaned.

"Come." It was an order. The one she followed without protest. Every time. She submitted and walked toward him, scissors in hand. When she got to the edge of the tub, he pulled her into the water. She sat between his legs, leaning her back against his chest. "Give me the scissors." She passed them, and to her surprise, she felt his hands in her hair. She looked over her shoulder.

"You know what you're doing?" she asked.

"Nah, but you can tell me. Shit can't be rocket science, right?" he asked.

She smirked. "Just find the thread near my scalp and cut. Only the thread, and carefully," she instructed.

Ethic went to work, as she leaned against him. She couldn't believe he was helping her with this.

"Why'd you put this in your hair?" he asked.

She shrugged.

"Don't do that," he said. "We not keeping things from one another. Why'd you choose this style? Those shoes?"

"Being with you feels high-maintenance," she said. "Felt like I needed to look the part."

Ethic kept cutting. "If I wanted that, I would choose that. I chose you. I want you. If you want the weave, I'm with it. If you want it. If you like it. I ain't the man to tell a woman how to be a woman but be the type of woman *you* want to be. Not the type you think I want, because all I want is you."

She was silent for the next 30 minutes, as he figured out how to remove all the muddy tracks from her hair.

When all she had were cornrows left, she turned to him. "This what you want?"

"Nah, I can do without the Cleo joints," he said, with a handsome smirk. Alani splashed him, as her laughter turned that smirk into a full-blown smile. She unraveled the braids and then he put his hands in her hair. "Like this," he said, as he dug all in her scalp. "I want you just like this."

He washed the mud from her body and handled his business last, before getting out. She stood in front of him, natural, short, shrunken curls, and all smiles. He wrapped her in a plush towel and then kissed her lips.

"Yo, we got to put on some clothes before I lose my restraint," he said. Not a single word was a joke.

He followed her into the bedroom. Ethic appreciated the seclusion of this farm house. It protected their love, trapped their insecurities and allowed them to flourish... allowed them to leave everything that hindered them back in the city, four hours away. He had envisioned a woman there when he had purchased it. He had pictured long nights filled with deep conversation on the porch swing. It sat on the edge of Lake Erie, miles and miles away from another soul. No one would ever find them, if they didn't want them too. It was like their own world where they didn't have to apologize for working things out. They could love freely without judgement, even the self-imposed conflict that he knew Alani suffered from. She never spoke of it, but he wasn't naïve enough to think it had just dissipated. It existed. She was just polite enough to not vocalize it.

The silk camisole and tiny, silk, boy shorts Alani put on was more enticing than bare skin.

"Are you hungry?" she asked. "Is there food here?"

"I could eat," he answered. "I had the kitchen stocked before we came up. I'll make something."

She shook her head. "Let me," she said. "You can keep me company if you'd like." She tiptoed out of the room. He slid into boxer briefs and sweat pants, before he followed the noise she was producing from his kitchen.

He stood in the threshold, leaning against the wall, arms crossed, as he admired her. She had music playing from her cell phone that sat on the center island.

Baby, it breaks my heart…
To think that loving me is not easy to do…

"You're into love songs. Nineties music," he said, as he finessed his lips. Another nuance of dating. Another lesson in all things Alani. He was learning her preferences. The simple ones.

"Mostly," she said, as she pulled eggs from the refrigerator. "A lot of the songs are about heartbreak. I can relate."

Ethic nodded.

"And now, I'm in love with someone. Real love that I'd die before losing. The rest of the songs are about that. I can relate to that too."

Her words made him go warm inside. They were reassurance. He didn't know how she had become the person in his life that made things feel solid, but somehow with just words, she comforted what had ailed him his entire life. As long as he had her, everything would be alright. She provided security in a different form than what most people valued. Emotional equity. She supplied him with something money couldn't buy. "Lucky man."

She looked at him in the eyes. "I should have been better to you, Ethic, before…I was so horrible to you. You should have walked out a long time ago but you're here and you're loving me, even after I was so cruel. I can be mean. I've always been that way. It stops people from trying to get close and it stops me from letting them in; because once people get in…once men get in…" she paused and shook her head, closing her eyes. "They hurt me. I'm sorry for being mean and hateful toward you. I'm not proud of that."

She was taking accountability for the part she had played in their brokenness. Her eyes glistened with emotion because this was hard for her...admitting her wrongs...she wasn't a woman who did so easily, but everything she had done in relationships hadn't worked. This time around, she would do the opposite...what she had done before had made men leave, so this time, she would move differently to get this man...this king...to stay.

"Don't apologize to me, Lenika. Don't apologize for your womanhood. The ups. The downs. The flux of emotions. The moods. You're a woman. That's what you're designed to do. To feel shit. You feel what you must, when you must. You weren't with men before. You chose boys. I'm a man..." he paused and approached her, capturing her face in his hands. Even the feeling of his fingertips on her skin felt glorious. Her lids lowered, as he commanded her stare. Alani couldn't breathe. He made her so nervous, filled her with such anxiety...he was so potent...so intoxicating... "I'm your man and I'll make you 'un-feel' all that shit."

She blushed and released all the tension she felt, in a sigh. She was always so emotional with him. He made her bleed sentiment. He tasted her lips, a soft kiss, and she nestled her head right in his chest, wrapping her arms around his back. She loved their every interaction, but this one, a simple hug, would always be her favorite. His embrace was legendary... life-changing...in his arms she felt safe. She heard the growl of his stomach and she pulled back, reluctant to let him go, but comforted because she knew there were no more limits on his love. She could always go back for more. He had a need she could fill. He was starving. She would feed him.

"I feel like eating breakfast. Is that cool?"

"Whatever you want is fine," he said.

"I know you're a healthy eater and all," she said. "Why wouldn't you tell me that? I know the first time I cooked for you, your stomach was tore up!" she laughed, smiling wide, as the carefree look on her face moved Ethic on the inside. He shook his head, smiling. He couldn't remember the last time he had smiled so much. She had him out here like a love-sick teenager, enjoying his first time with a girl on his arm.

"Well, I like bacon. Real, greasy, fat covered bacon." She laughed at the grimace that spread across his face. "I'll make you a veggie omelet, baby."

Baby. There she went with those damn arrows. He placed a hand over the left side of his chest, rubbing, as he licked his lips. He could bypass the omelet in that moment. He had an appetite for something else.

"That'll do," he replied.

"You think we should call and check on the kids?" she asked.

Damn. She had a whole arsenal of arrows. Where the fuck was she pulling them from? She was relentlessly aiming for his heart. Might as well call her cupid. When Alani was happy, she radiated energy. She made his spirit glow. He told himself he had to keep her this way. He wrapped his arms around her waist. He held her from behind, burying his lips in the crook of her neck, as she continued to dice onions and peppers.

"They're fine. They know to call if they need me," he said.

"Maybe we should have brought them," she countered. "I mean, this place just feels like a family is meant to fill these walls. It probably would have been good for Mo."

Fuck, she was wetting shit up. Spraying effortlessly. Arrows every fucking where. She had referred to the five of them as family...not friends, not kindred spirits...but a family...a singular unit that moved in conjunction with one another... that loved one another...fought for one another. She wanted to be a part of his clan. "I saw paddle boats out by the dock. They would have had so much fun."

"How do you love them so much?" he asked. The question came out foreign, like he had put his words together incorrectly, but she knew exactly what he meant. How? Not, why. How could Alani love his children so purely? He had to know.

"They're important to me. When I couldn't have you, they gave me pieces of you. They restore my motherhood, Ethic. That Bella..." she paused and shook her head, as she smiled. "She loved me even when I didn't deserve it. She never thought twice. Never hated me for hurting you," she whispered. "She's such a beautiful girl. Her energy..." Alani felt a chill run down her spine and she shivered. Just the thought of Bella made her eyes mist. "You've really done a great job raising her alone..." She moved onto rinsing the mushrooms, then put those under her blade as well. Ethic swayed her in his hold, not far, just a slight rock back and forth while she diced, and he listened to her praise his children. "…and Eazy…" she scoffed. "I've never had a boy. Boys and their mothers..." She shook her head. "They say there is no deeper bond. If it's anything like the love he gives to me, I understand. When he barrels into me and wraps his arms around me, I just melt. He makes me feel needed."

"You are needed, Lenika," he said. "Thank you for loving them the way you do. I never thought I'd trust a woman with them. Never thought I could trust *anyone* with them, in fact. Even when they're at school, it's this gnawing in my gut, like I got to stay ready to fuck shit up just in case someone hurts them. You've changed that. I've never felt like I had to protect them from you."

She stretched her neck to look back at him and he kissed her nose.

"I know I'm not their mother, but I want to be something. I don't know where I fit, but I just want to fit," she admitted. She looked down in embarrassment because she knew she was moving too fast and revealing the hurt that still weighed on her. "Or maybe I'm just desperate to be somebody's mother. I miss that part of my life." She pulled in a deep breath. "I'm sorry for bringing it up," she said, as she exhaled and tried to shake away everything she was feeling. He turned her toward him.

"You can bring it up. You can talk to me about that and anything else, even if it's hard. Even if it's uncomfortable. I know what we have to work through. I know what goes through your head," he said, as he tapped her temple, gently, with two fingers. "Don't keep it there. Let it out, as often as you need to," he said. He gripped her face and she nodded, closing her eyes to seal the emotion that filled her eyes inside.

"I'm going to go upstairs. I'm kind of tired. Is that okay?" She whispered. Alani was barely keeping it together and she was desperate for a bit of privacy, so she could gather herself. Ethic stepped back, giving her space. He lifted his hands in surrender and Alani bolted. She rushed for the stairs but halted at the edge of the kitchen. She gripped her stomach and folded her lips inside her mouth to stop the sob from fleeing. "Ethic?"

"Yeah?"

She couldn't turn to him because he would see her tears. He would see the guilt she felt for loving him. She sniffed. "I'm not running away from you. I'm not leaving. I just need a minute. Okay?"

Ethic was silent, as he watched her. Her neck bowed so disgracefully, despite the fact that she was the most graceful woman he had ever met. The sins in the room were his to bear, but just like a good woman, she was adopting them, finding fault in herself when it was he whom had fucked up. He wanted to comfort her, but she needed space. It was so hard for Ethic to oblige because he just wanted her near. As much time as they had spent apart, he had anxiety whenever she disappeared for too long. He feared one day he would look away and when he turned back to her she would be gone…like he was a dying man in a desert and a mirage of her had given him reprieve only to disappear before his very eyes. "Okay," he replied.

Her feet on the wooden staircase sounded like a stampede,

as she raced up them. Ethic dragged a slow hand over his face and sat. His eyes fell on her open tote bag, the one Bella had insisted on buying Alani last Christmas. Her manuscript sat inside. He hesitated, before reaching for it, but curiosity urged him to pick up the pages. He was desperate to get inside her head, because although she was keeping up a strong front, he knew she was broken inside. He could hear her, stifling her cries upstairs. Going to her felt instinctual, staying on the first level of the home felt respectful.

The Ethic of Love.

Something inside him splintered when he realized her book was about him. He flipped the page and began to read, bracing himself for what was to come.

-He captured my soul the first day he set eyes on me and I haven't been free since.

-His touch sets me on fire. No matter if by hatred or love. I'm always set ablaze by him. It's the best and worst thing I've ever felt in my life. So explosive.

-I love him so much that even when I hate him I still pray for him.

-The universe took my daughter and gave me him. Somehow, the transference of energy feels equal.

-There is no such thing as wrong love.

-I can finally admit to loving him. Every fiber of his being I adore. Even the killer he keeps dormant inside, because he's motivated by love, never hate.

-I can survive with this sadness inside, as long as he's next to me.

-I want to die without him because with him life is dark,

without him I'm blind.

Some of the passages slit him right down the middle and left his insides at his feet on the floor. The book was heavy. It suffocated him slowly and he understood now how she had developed the nerve to turn a gun on herself and pull the trigger. All of this had been inside her, festering, rotting her, depressing her. He sat there for hours, flipping through page after page until the words...

There is no end, not with us. There is only a new beginning. Every time we're even close to ending, I'll start over with him again, chasing a new outcome, a new destiny, because I'm a woman in love. I'll endure the pain forever, before I ever allow this to end.

CHAPTER 16

Bella sat, watching Nannie sleep in her recliner, as the news played on the television screen. Eazy's head rested in her lap and she slid her thumb down the iPhone screen. Nighttime was noisy on the Northside of Flint. It wasn't like in the suburbs. All she heard outside her window at home were crickets. At Nannie's, the streets came alive at night.

The boisterous sounds of Connie and her friends playing cards right in the front yard echoed through the air. The smack of the basketball hitting the pavement was loud. The smell of barbecue permeated right through the front door.

Bella lifted Eazy's head and slowly inched from beneath him, taking extra caution not to wake him. She cringed, as she took timid steps towards the front door. Every single floorboard seemed to creak along the way. Bella clenched her teeth, as she pulled open the door and slid her body out.

The cool air felt like freedom.

Bella stuffed her hands into the pockets of her Gucci cardigan, as she posted up on the bottom step.

"Ugh! No, this girl can't turn! I get a do-over. I can't jump right if the rope sloppy!"

A group of girls stood in the middle of the street, barefoot on the dirty pavement, as a brown girl with long, tribal braids stood on the curb with her hands on her hips. The street lights shone right over them and the rope they turned ticked against the concrete in a cadence.

Tribal girl jumped into the rope and it tangled, instantly.

"Get off the rope, Drea! You can't turn for me!"

The girl looked around and her eyes fell on Bella. "Yo, you know how to turn double Dutch?"

Bella shrugged. "Not really. I've never played," she admitted.

"Well, you got to be better than this girl. Come turn," the girl said. "Unless you want to hug the porch all night. You Lenika's cousin or something?"

Bella stood and walked over to the game. "She's my stepmom," Bella said, without thinking twice.

"Since when she get married? My mama said her mean-ass gon' be single forever," the girl said, laughing, as the other girls chuckled to.

"She's not single. My daddy the one who bought her your mother's house," Bella said, with a shrug and smirk.

"Okay, you got it, bougie-ass," the girl said, turning up her nose. "You turning or what?" The girl snatched the ropes from another girl and handed them to Bella.

Bella widened her stance and began to turn along with the girl standing across from her.

Little Ms. Tribal Braids jumped into the rope.

"What's your name anyway?" the girl panted, as she jumped.

"Bella."

"What kind of name is that? Ol' white girl name? You talk white too. Dress all fancy. What school you go to?"

"Grand Blanc," Bella answered.

The girl did all types of tricks inside the ropes and Connie came over to the curb. "Aye! What y'all youngins know about double Dutch?" she challenged. She jumped into the rope, gut and butt bouncing everywhere, as she took a turn with her daughter. Bella laughed, as the adults in the yard cheered Connie on. When the ropes finally tangled, Connie waved them out the street. "Come get y'all some food before it's all gone," she said.

Bella turned back towards Nannie's house.

"You can come too, baby, come get you a plate," Connie said.

Bella stopped, glanced up at the house, wondering if she should just leave well enough alone and sneak back inside.

"Yo, bougie, you coming?" the girl asked.

Bella backpedaled and then turned toward the loudmouth girl to run and catch up. Nannie slept like a rock. As long as she was back before five o'clock in the morning when Nannie normally started her day, Bella would be fine.

"I'm Lyric," the girl said, as they stepped up to the table that was set up directly in front of the front steps to stop people from going into Connie's front door. The food was laid out in aluminum pans. "That's Shayla and Bianca." She nodded to the other girls who were all grabbing paper plates.

"Hey," Bella greeted.

"That's all yo' hair?" Bianca asked.

Bella finessed her long ponytail. "Yeah, it's mine," she answered.

"It's cute. Better braid that shit up out here. One fight and you getting dog walked with all that," Bianca added.

"One fight and my daddy shooting this whole block up," Bella shot back.

"Who you think yo' daddy is? You ain't even from around here," Shayla said. "He probably some square."

"Nah, her daddy ain't no square."

The voice came from behind them and Bella turned around, frowning, because someone was speaking on her father...someone she was sure didn't know him at all.

"You Ethic daughter, right? He the only nigga riding through the hood in a Tesla without getting pulled out that bitch. Niggas know better. That's your pops, right?"

Bella couldn't find her voice. The boy standing in front of her had peanut butter skin, fresh faded sides, with a middle part and two braids to the back. She was stuck and staring. He smirked, then licked his lips. She noticed the tiny scar above his top lip, it bubbled slightly, and was barely noticeable, but was the cutest thing Bella had ever seen. Her heart fluttered.

"Y'all better be careful out here with her. One thing happen to her and dear daddy hanging niggas from the street lights," he said, as he backpedaled.

"Ain't nothing gon' happen to her, boy! These hoes know not to start no shit over here. Everybody out here family," Lyric said. "You good out here, girl, don't listen to Hendrix."

Hendrix...

Bella was already practicing his name in bubble letters with glitter markers inside her mind.

"Y'all coming to the kickback? We about to breakout," he said.

"Yeah, we coming around the back though cuz my mama gon' trip if she see us walk off with y'all," Lyric shot back.

"Bet," he said.

Hendrix reached into Bella's plate and took a potato chip from it, stuffing it into his mouth, before backpedaling back toward the group of boys that sat across the street posted on the porch.

"He so fine," Shayla said, shaking her head.

"You coming, Bougie?" Lyric asked.

"Yeah, I guess that's cool," Bella said. She knew if she got caught, Ethic would never let her out of his sight again, but no way was she not going. It was like the cute boy in the Jordan sweat suit had cast a spell on her.

"Ma, we going to the store. We'll be back," Lyric called.

Connie was busy on the card table and gave her permission with a wave of her hand.

"Come on," Lyric said, leading the way through the backyard. Bella looked back at Nannie's one time, before slipping through the hole in the fence.

"How old are you, Bougie?" Lyric asked.

"Thirteen," she said. Her first lie. She was 12, but in her young mind, adding that one year made her seem more mature.

"You smoke?" Bianca asked.

"Not with everybody," Bella answered. It was true. She

197

had tried weed before, once, when Daphne Parker had brought some to school and they had snuck behind the bleachers to smoke. She had enjoyed the high…enjoyed forgetting about her worries of being a motherless child, of being the middle one. Mo got most of the attention because of her circumstances and Eazy was the youngest and Ethic's prized gift from Raven. The weed had made her forget, but it had also stayed in her hair for hours. She'd had to wash it as soon as she got home, just so her dad never found out.

"We ain't everybody. We your people. You gon' need people if you gon' be coming around the way, rocking Gucci without getting that shit snatched," Lyric said.

"I'm not really worried about that," Bella said.

"You think yo' daddy big shit, huh, bougie?" Lyric asked, with a chuckle.

Bella shrugged. She didn't think that. She knew that. She was realizing how much weight her father's name carried, how much respect he received, and she knew why.

Because he's a killer.

The thought used to scare her. It no longer did. She didn't like it, but after what Cream had done to Alani, Bella understood that sometimes there were consequences to actions…when dealing with her father, those consequences were severe. She had lost a sibling and she had a feeling that Cream had lost his life behind that. She felt no qualms about it.

"Okayyy," Lyric joked. They approached an abandoned house and Bella heard the sounds of music coming from behind the tan boards covering the doors and windows. Lyric pulled back the board to the front door and slid inside.

Bella frowned, as she stepped inside. Graffiti covered the walls, trash littered the floor but it was packed. Weed smoke and the sound of Big Sean filled the air. Candles lit the space.

"You guys hang out here?" Bella asked.

"Yeah, nobody bothers us. We can swerve without my mama nosy-ass hating," Lyric said.

"Swerve?" Bella frowned, in confusion.

"Smoke, drink, just do whatever we want…no eyes on us. Just complete freedom."

Bella got that part…the freedom part. Being Ethic's child had a way of feeling like being imprisoned. He was so afraid of losing; so concerned with death that he smothered them a bit. It was why she enjoyed coming to Nannie's. It was emancipation. Bella could travel the blocks out of her sight, as long as the street lights didn't beat her home. Nannie had grown up in the hood, so there wasn't much that scared her, and she knew everyone on the block. Bella was free to roam, but never after dark, never this late. She checked her phone, discovering that it was nearing midnight. She knew Nannie was still sleeping, because had she discovered Bella's absence, her phone would have been blowing up by now.

"You want something to drink?" Lyric asked.

Bella shook her head. Her heart was pounding. Anxiety crawled through her bones, as she took in the faces in the darkened room. Teenagers of all ages, parlaying, chilling, playing grown, when really, they didn't even know what being grown entailed. It was an entirely different world than the one Ethic had raised her in. She was a lion cub that had made her way to the wild. She would either thrive and build a kingdom or die. There was no in between.

Lyric and the girls sparked up, causing Bella to fan the smoke away from her. No way would she be able to walk back into Nannie's house smelling like Kush. "I'm going to get some air," she said.

Lyric nodded, as she pinched the joint between her lips and inhaled until the tip turned orange.

Bella turned sideways, easing through the thickening crowd, and then pushed the cardboard aside to exit.

"Running back to the 'burbs already?"

The question was awaiting her, as soon as she touched the first step. She turned to find Hendrix sitting off to the side of the porch - alone.

"I'm not running," she answered back. He scoffed and leaned forward to his knees.

"How old are you, anyway?" he asked.

"Fourteen," she lied.

"How old are you really?" he said, with a lazy smile.

"I'll be 13 in three months," she whispered. For some reason, it sounded better than 12. Twelve sounded childish. "How old are you?"

"Years don't matter with somebody like me. With the stuff I've seen, I might as well be an old man out here," Hendrix said.

"Well, if that's the way you're counting, I'm old out here too," she mumbled.

Bella shrank under his scrutiny, as he took her in. "It's rude to stare," she said, lifting her eyes to stare right back.

"Stop doing it then, nigga," Hendrix shot back.

She bit into her bottom lip and looked toward the street to stop him from seeing through her. She liked him, and she had a feeling that he knew that she liked him. She had a feeling that a lot of girls liked him and that he didn't like very many back. Her stomach hollowed, and the palms of her hands dewed. Bella could barely breathe, she was so nervous.

"A girl like you ain't even supposed to be out here," Hendrix stated.

"Like me?" Bella asked. She wondered what he saw when he looked at her. What did that mean? What type of girl was she? Was it the type he liked?

"Yeah," he said. "Good. Nobody around here has that. Ain't none of us out here innocent. We're all wolves. Even Lyric and 'em. We're all bad. It's just in us. We the bottom. We so low they trying to poison us out. We ain't worth nothing, ain't got nothing, not even clean water to drink. You don't belong here. You come here because you think it's fun. This partying and bullshitting seem fun and it is when you're not from around here, but for us, it's the only way to escape. For all of us, this is a trap."

Bella didn't know how to respond. She couldn't pretend to know what it felt like to be in his shoes. She had always had the best of everything. She had never worked for anything a day of her life. She certainly didn't know deprivation, but she knew loss. She was a girl who had gone without a mother for the majority of her life. Alani made it easier. Alani was changing that, but she would never forget the years she had gone feeling like a motherless child. Those years had hurt. She had been trapped, not by poverty, but by abandonment... she was trapped by the secret resentment she held against a dead woman. Bella hated her mother for not being strong enough to escape the man that had killed her, and she had never been brave enough to admit that to anyone. Then, out of nowhere, Alani had come along and loved that resentment away. She had shown Bella a love that she was missing. Filled the most painful void, as if it had never been there at all.

"Maybe you just need someone to show you a way out," Bella said. He stood from his seat and approach her. He towered over Bella's small frame, long and lanky, with tattoos and barely-there facial hair, she tried to guess his age. She wasn't sure why she was holding her breath. He made her feel like she would pass out...like she was dizzy, and if she tried to walk away, she would embarrass herself and fall. Her throat tightened in anxiety and her mouth dried. She had liked a boy before, but it had felt nothing like this. A car pulled up to the curb and a boy wearing a red bandana around his head hung half way out the window. "Yo, Dri, nigga, what up?"

Hendrix looked down at Bella and then rolled eyes out to the car full of young men.

"Can't show me the way out if you're here too," he said. "Go home before your pops come through and shut the whole block down," he said. He bumped her slightly, as he slid by her. He was rude, arrogant, and he took those steps in such a cool swagger that Bella couldn't tear her eyes away.

When he bent over to climb into the car, his hoodie lifted slightly, revealing the handle of a chrome pistol. Bella's heart quickened. Bad boys just did something to good girls. It was the way of the hood...it never failed. She turned to go back inside, but before she could even lift the cardboard covering the door, she heard...

"Yo, Pretty Girl!"

She turned to see his face come into view, as the back window rolled down.

"Home is that way," he stated, pointing down the block. "Go home."

The car pulled away, and for some reason, Bella listened. She tucked her hands in her back pockets and descended the steps, headed back to Nannie's, with thoughts of Hendrix running through her mind.

CHAPTER 17

Ethic's heart raged like a river, flowing downstream.
His emotions flooded everything, as he made his
way up the stairs. He was sure she was asleep by
now. The sun would be rising soon. It had taken him
all night to read her work, some pages he'd read twice, to
fully absorb the impact of her words. It was a story about the
fairness of love. Were there rules to it? Had they broken them?
He wasn't sure, but he knew one thing, he had shattered
her. He entered the bedroom and the silhouette of her frame
could be seen beneath the sheets. She laid on her side with
her back to him and he eased into the bed. He wrapped one
arm around her and she stirred, as she pulled his hand close
to her chest, intertwining her fingers with his, then making a
combined fist. He kissed the back of her neck.

"Ethic?" Her voice was as clear as day. She hadn't slept. She
had been lying there for hours, overthinking.

"Hmm," he huffed.

"I can't sleep. My mind is racing. There's this hole that
I feel sometimes. Right in the center of me. I need you to
fill me, because right now, I'm so empty," she whispered. "I
need to feel you." He thought of Morgan in that moment. She
had talked about feeling holes inside too, and he wondered

if every man that had ever hurt a woman, intentional or not, dug a new one. How could women walk around so strong if they were hollow on the inside? It nagged at his gut. "I need you inside me," Alani whispered.

"But Nyair-"

"Fuck Nyair," Alani shot back. "I need it."

"You need it, baby?" he whispered, pressing into her, growing at the thought, as he hardened against her softness.

"Yes," she panted. He gripped the base of his need and rubbed the tip against her behind. Expert hands peeled down those shorts and he planted a kiss on her shoulder.

She felt his warmth against her, as his strength split her southern lips. He gripped her left breast, as his dick entered wet walls. His lips to the back of her neck accompanied the thrust that divided her. He fucked her, on her side, so thick, so long that he touched her depths, even in this loving position. She turned her neck to see him, gripping the back of his head, as she struggled to kiss his lips. God, she just wanted to taste him. It wasn't in the way he fucked her, it was in the way he held her, gripping her, flesh to flesh, with desperation, as if he was afraid to let go.

"Hmm," he groaned. "I missed you, baby," he whispered. His fist balled in hers, was over her heart, as he thrust in and out. She felt every muscle in his body, flexing, working, to bring her pleasure. The subtle moans he tried to stifle lived in her ear, as he repositioned himself, turning her on her stomach as he stroked from behind.

The way he licked her back, while stroking her slow, had Alani climbing the walls, whining so softly that it sounded like she was crying. There was no pain in this room, however, this was all pleasure, this was well earned and long overdue. The mental and spiritual awakening happening in her…and more importantly, in him, would lead them to orgasm. His strong thighs were spread so wide, giving him leverage as he dug for her treasure. His stroke was so passionate, so slow, with a little bit of thug at the very end of each pump, when he popped the back of her pussy with aggression. Ethic was taking her body for a ride and all she could do was hold on tight.

"I'm about to cum. Ezra!" she screamed. She panicked when she felt him stop moving. It was like someone had tossed her into the deep end of the pool. "No! No, Ethic, please. God, keep going." There was no doubt about it. She was begging for this dick. He was stroking her, balls deep, making her take it all, before pulling out to the tip and then diving in again.

"I just want to take my time with you, baby," Ethic whispered, going still because if he kept at this pace he was going to explode. He wanted to relish in this. He wanted to take his time with this plate. Savor the taste. Eat it in courses, then beat so good he put her to sleep. "Be patient with me."

The words that fell from this man's tongue. Patience was a virtue, one that Alani didn't possess. They had been apart for almost a year and they had so much love making to catch up on. Ethic was the type of man you made love to every night…they had missed too many nights and Alani wanted to play catch up. She had been lonely, full of hurt and burden for so long. She had been ashamed to love him, but in this bedroom, under the roof that he provided, the roof that he wanted her to live under with him, she finally felt peace. She felt him. Ethic had a way of turning night to morning, and as he made magic of her body, she just held on tight. He brought her to tears. It felt so fucking good. God, he was amazing. How the hell was he this amazing? A fucking marvel of a man... designed to bring her to orgasm. Alani was thirsty, from exhaustion, as she tried to keep up. Her throat dried, and her moans ran out of her, raspy, as she threw her sex back at him, while he took her from behind. Alani couldn't keep up. He popped that thang like his life depended on it, like her love depended on it, like if he didn't make her feel that ache in the back of her depths when a nigga went a little too hard, she would leave him. Ethic had her spinning. Alani wasn't sure what was up or down, as he dug into the meat of the back of her thighs with his fingertips. He was the best sex she had ever had and each time it got better, like he trained for this shit. Like he went home and played back the game tapes to make sure he made the three-point shot next time.

What the fuck?

Alani knew she was ugly. The way her face twisted up from absolute pleasure, she couldn't worry about looking sexy. She was just trying to take it, gritting her teeth and biting her tongue to handle it.

What the entire fuck?

Alani would kill him. Shoot him dead and not miss this time, if he ever, motherfucking ever, even thought about giving this dick to anyone else. It was hers. She was staying.

Fuck everybody who thought otherwise, and fuck Nyair's holy-ass too for trying to keep her from this pleasure. They could start their own religion because this man was a god. Ethic made her delirious. She couldn't think straight when he was inside her. It was a crazy she welcomed. A delusion she enjoyed. This black, burnt, yoga practicing, patience having, perfect father being, pussy-slaying-ass nigga was fucking the shit out of Alani and she was sold. She was his. She didn't care how many tears she had to cry in the bathroom behind closed doors. She would never leave dick like this. She had paid for it in pain and the receipt of her heart said non-refundable.

The grumble in the back of his throat every time he connected with the back of her let her know he was close. It let her know she was the shit.

"Ethic, waaaaait," she moaned. "Please."

He slowed.

"What are you doing? I'll kill you if you stop," she threatened, as her arms spread wide at her sides, her nails clutching the sheets.

"Patience," he groaned.

SLAP

Her right ass cheek stung, as he shortened his stroke. Alani whimpered, like she was injured, and she was…he was beating that thang. Beating it like a drum. Beating it like he was dressed in African cloth and there were bare-footed dancers in the room. My fucking…

"Godddd!"

Alani came. Hard. Harder than she ever had before. She had lost the fight. She felt the folds of her flesh pulsing. Yep, he had beat that shit all the way up. It was throbbing. She felt wetness gush from her, all over him.

"Damn," he whispered, as he gripped both of her cheeks and massaged them in a circle, making them go 'round and 'round on his dick because he was still inside her and the visual of her ass, with the slightly lighter stretch marks, moving over the black rod that parted her... "God, damn."

This nigga here.

Even the sound of his voice made her swoon.

He pulled out and she felt hollow.

Do a bitch got any walls left?

He came up her body, hovering over her, as she laid there on her stomach. He kissed the back of her neck. "Hmm," she moaned.

"I'm sorry," he whispered. "For everything you've felt besides this. For everything I've given you that wasn't love."

This nigga here.

Ethic was a whole man. Most had a way with words, some paid bills well, some laid the pipe, others you felt protected around, some men made you laugh. Ethic did it all. He had a way with everything. He left no opportunity for another man to make her feel something that he didn't provide. He gave her his all.

Where did he even come from? Where did they make his particular model? This type? Could bitches order one up on Amazon? Because Amazon had every fucking thing. She would Amazon Prime the fuck out of this nigga if she could. Nah, it didn't have nothing like this. He was out-of-stock, one of one, a rare collector's edition, and he was hers.

Alani turned to him, fighting her fatigue, as he went onto his back. Alani mounted him. He was much like that Mustang. She was afraid to saddle him, fearful that she couldn't tame his wild...that he would buck her off, but she was a glutton for punishment. She slid down onto him. He was like the stake you stuck into the ground when you pitched a tent, to keep it grounded. He rooted her. He kept her from blowing away in the wind. Alani leaned down and kissed him. Sloppy kisses. Desperate kisses. Let me swallow your black-ass whole type kisses. She moved her hips slowly, adjusting to his width because he filled her, every inch. Thick-ass. Long-ass. Ethic's dick was perfection and she rode that thing. Up. Down. Circles. Bounce a little.

He reached up and placed his hands on her breasts, and then brought her down so that he could taste them. Kissing one, then the other, biting one, then the other, flicking one, then the other. Pushing them together and then sucking both.

THIS NIGGA HERE!

He lifted his pelvis to meet her halfway because she was Ethic's woman and Ethic's woman simply didn't do all the work by herself. Never would he ever let that happen. Alani might as well had been skating, like an old-school 90's rink, gliding from side to side on that thang because they had found a rhythm.

"Ethic, I can't take it," she groaned, as she closed her eyes and laid against his chest, as she came again, before him, again. The stamina of this man was incredible.

"Two for one, baby," he whispered, as he wrapped both arms around her back and then kissed her shoulder. Alani cried. Like real tears. Like sobbed and not in pain. It was just too much pleasure. Everybody knew too much chocolate made your tummy ache, but just like a fat kid with cake, Alani wanted more. He was still inside her and she was leaking all over him.

Round 3...

Alani Hill in one corner, black eyes, busted lip, clinging to the ropes. She could barely stand. Ethic Okafor in the other, bobbing and weaving, as he threw practice jabs in her direction. Unaffected. The motherfucking people's champ; nah, scratch that...the motherfucking pussy champ.

Fuck it. She was going back into the ring. He would have to knock her out to get the title because there was not an ounce of bitch in her. She wouldn't quit. Even if she was losing. She would get in this ring with him again and again, go round for round. Nothing less than the knockout would take her down.

Alani only knew one advantage she had over him, and as she lifted, she felt flutters of confidence flutter in her stomach. She lowered her head into his lap and she felt him tense, as one hand gripped the top of her head. Alani took him into her mouth without reserve, like the juices covering him was toppings of a FroYo cone, because she was trying to lose a couple pounds, so ice cream was a no-go. The way he slid to the back of her throat and gripped her desperately, tensing beneath her, toes cracking as they curled, made Alani go harder. Her hands were cold, so she placed them under his ass, warming them, while forcing him deeper down her throat.

"Fucccck." She knew she was doing her job because Ethic wasn't very vocal during sex, unless he couldn't help it. When her hands lost their chill, she wrapped them around him and rotated, like she was grinding pepper. She slobbered all over him, focusing on the light-skinned part of his wide head. She tugged up, then down, while her wrists went to work. "Fuckkk!"

Checkmate, nigga.

She felt his orgasm, as it rose from the base of him and pulsed all the way to the top. Alani had developed a taste for him the very first time she had wrapped her lips around him, and she didn't pull back. She swallowed him, not daring to waste a drop, like his nut was made of truffles, because everybody knew you didn't waste that expensive shit.

"Fuckkk," he reacted. She had stolen the rest of his vocabulary. She climbed him, laying directly on top of him, as he wrapped her in a cocoon of security. His arms covered by a blanket. A kiss to the top of her head.

"We don't have to tell Nyair. We'll just start over in the morning. A do-over. We just needed to get it out our systems one last time," she whispered.

"Yup," he groaned. "Start fresh in the morning," he agreed, in a sleepy drawl. They both desperately wanted to get this counseling thing right, but damn, it was hard to stay disconnected from one another. Sexually was where they performed best. She felt the soothing stroke of his hand against her back and her eyes closed. Knocked out. The bout was over, and just like that, the emptiness she felt was filled.

CHAPTER 18

Alani groaned, as she lifted her head slightly. She was stuck to Ethic. Neither had moved in hours and she had to peel her skin from his, as she awoke from the slumber. The taste of dick was on her breath and a little bit of pussy. She gagged, as she climbed from the bed, hearing Nannie's voice in her head. *"Don't think I don't know you out here hunching. Coming in here with 'dussy' all on your breath,"* she used to fuss. Alani had to stifle a laugh because she had never known what Nannie meant until this very moment. She definitely reeked of both and she tiptoed to the bathroom, taking extra care not to wake him. The shower felt amazing, as the water pressure rained down over her. Alani wished she'd brought hair products. Now that the weave was out, her wash and go would be unruly because she had nothing to define her curls, not even a ponytail holder to tie her hair back. She let the night's sins go down the drain, before stepping out. She brushed her teeth and then slipped into leggings and a tank before creeping out of the room. It felt glorious to leave him there, sleeping, resting, because she knew all she had to do was turn right back to be underneath him. They had never had that...the promise of tomorrow. They always loved one another in doses, taking in as much of each other in one night because when the sun rose, it shined down on their shame, causing them to flee. This time was different. This time she could stay, and it felt glorious. Alani grabbed the keys to Ethic's car and walked out to grab her yoga mat. She turned to head back to the house when the sound of the waves washing gently ashore garnered her attention. This farm was truly peace on Earth. She didn't even know how Ethic had found it. She had never thought about the Northern, more secluded parts of Michigan. All she had known was the hood. This part of the state was beautiful, and she wouldn't mind staying forever…with him, the seclusion would feel like a gift. She made her way to the edge of the water and spread the mat out. The sun beamed over her, as the sound of crickets sounded in the distance. Such natural peace. She would burn up out here under the sun, but it somehow felt like the perfect place to meditate. She slipped out of her flip flops, kicked off her yoga pants and shed her top. She tested the water's temperature. It was brisk, and she didn't dare dip anything other than a toe inside. The water gave its own soundtrack, as she began her daily routine. She felt free, as the air kissed her skin. She felt uninhibited. Like the struggle that had weighed her down was finally lifting or she was just getting stronger, strong enough to beat whatever devils were attacking her spirit. She was proud of the woman she was becoming. It was a slow transformation, but she was no longer discounting the strides she made. All movement was good, as long as it was forward. It was progress and she was proud of that.

Alani planted her palms into the mat, as she kept her pelvis to the ground and lifted up onto straight arms. *Vinyasa,* she thought, as she centered her breathing. In through her nose. Deep breathing. Hold. Hold some more. Control it. Feel it. Out through her mouth. She was breathing. She was living. *I'm fine. He's fine. We're okay.* She moved up into a downward dog, before bringing her right knee to her left elbow, feeling the stretch of her abs, as her body shook from the pressure it took to maintain that form. *Feel the struggle. Feel the hard moments. The burn. It hurts to hold this position too long. I'm not strong here. Fight for it anyway. Fight for him.* She lifted her right leg behind her, before lowering to the ground. *Vinyasa, down dog.* She could feel the tension leaving her, as she sucked in air through her nose and blew out hard through her mouth, expelling energy. Throwing away bullshit. Blocking the fuck shit. Her eyes were closed. She could feel the eradication. She was discharging negativity. Centering. Feeling nothingness. Then, she felt him. She felt him before he ever touched her. Ethic was an energy. A strike of lightning that set her body ablaze whenever he was around. She groaned, when she felt the hardness nestle right in the center of her behind. The cool air kissed her clitoris, as he slid her panties to the side. She wasn't cold long. His warm length parted her, from behind. He didn't ask because he didn't need to. Her body was his to partake in whenever he pleased.

"I tried, baby," he whispered.

Alani grit her teeth, sucking in air through parted lips, as her forehead wrinkled in satisfaction. Those eyes squeezed tighter. This feeling was delicious. It was edible.

"No," she whispered, whining. "We're connecting in other ways. We're supposed to be abstaining, Ethic. Last night was supposed to get it out our systems." Her words came out an octave higher.

He tensed into her again, stroking her deeper and her mouth fell open in bliss. He was so thick and long. He split her open so right that she felt like calling his name.

"You can't put this in front of me like this and expect me not to do something with it." His drawl was full of wanting. "You're all through my system, baby. Can't get rid of this shit."

He palmed a mound of her flesh before applying the sting of a smack, as he picked up his pace. He spread her open wider every time he went deep. It was the sweetest thing she had ever felt.

"Agh!" she cried. Her arms were at her side, lying flat against the mat and Ethic grabbed them, pulling on them, using them as reigns to pull her back onto his dick. She knew now why he brought her here. No one was around to hear her screams. This was an abduction. He had kidnapped her heart and was going to torture her in the sweetest way all weekend. His captor. He tensed into her so deeply that her stomach was flat on the ground. She was just lying there, whimpering, in absolute bliss, as he had his way with her. In the middle of the day, her passionate pleas echoing into the air, while her tears fell from her eyes. He loved her so much. She loved him even more. She was spent. Her body was sore, pussy throbbing, but she didn't want him to stop.

Couldn't bear it if he stopped. Alani wanted to see him, and just like Ethic to sense the need, he pulled out. "Come," he whispered.

She turned and crawled into his lap, fitting onto his dick like she was the puzzle piece he connected to. He gripped her curls and held her in place, as she rode him gently, while staring into his eyes.

"I want a life with you, Alani," he whispered. "I want to put life in you."

A streak of fear blazed through her. He was talking about a baby. A permanent link. There was still so much pain from the one she had loss. The one *they* had loss. He didn't know her history. He didn't know that her body wouldn't cooperate. If he wanted a baby with her, if he wanted to make another baby, and she couldn't give him one. The thought terrified her. Both the thought of birthing another, and of not being able to, scared her. It was that rock and hard thing predicament. She was in one of those and she wondered if she should tell him. Would he still want her? She was tainted fruit. He felt her shift of energy and he pulled back, gripping her face with one hand, staring into her eyes, curiously, as he kept guiding her down with the other. She blinked away the trepidation, hiding it behind lust, before he detected it.

Delicate fingers graced his face, as she gave him soft kisses while riding him. She made him feel like a king. He reminded her that she was a queen. This was perfection or as close to it as two lovers could get. Alani wrapped her arms around his neck, as her mouth parted. "I'm cumming, Ethic." She barely said it. It was a gasp on the tip of her tongue...she couldn't catch her breath. He leaned over her, putting her on her back, as he raced her to the finish line, causing her to tremor.

"This shit is amazing," he growled, as he buried his face in the nook of her neck. He pulled back, grabbing her feet, as his head fell back and he bit his lip, joining her there...at their favorite place. He stood and reached down for her. She took his hand and he pulled her to her feet before scooping her into his arms, and then heading for the water.

"You bet not!" she warned, as she held on tight. "Ethic, I swear to God if you drop me in this water..."

It was all she got out before he tossed her, then dove in himself.

"Agh!" the shock of the cold was exhilarating. She popped up and swept the water from her vision. "I'm going to kill you, boy!"

He smiled, a broad smile, a content smile. It was one she had never seen before and she loved, it as he swam to her. When he smiled like that, she heard birds chirping, like she was a real-life princess who had been saved by a prince...but no, this wasn't that story...this was real...she was a black woman who had been saved by Ezra "Ethic" Okafor and it was better than any fairy tale she had heard as a little girl. This man had loved her back to life, killed her with a complicated truth, then revived her again...they weren't perfect, but love wasn't supposed to be...it was supposed to be resilient... it was supposed to be strong...and everything about the two of them was exactly that. She wrapped her legs around his waist, as he stood in front of her, then he took her deeper. Further into the depths of this lake and his heart…always submerging her.

"I read your book," he admitted.

She tensed. "Some of that I wrote before…before we fixed things…it's not what I feel now…it's…"

"It's good," he said.

"Really?" she answered, in surprise. She'd thought he would be offended, or angry, or hurt. His understanding was shocking. Her eyes burned with emotion. The days she had spent writing those passages were dark. She had been drowned in hatred and grief. She had wanted to cut it out, to just bleed it out…her ink was the blood and it had spilled freely until it had killed the grief…murdered the depression and it was all about him…all about what they had been through and he liked it. How could he like it? How could he be so supportive that he was able to read the pain he had caused without taking offense? Ethic was built different than any man she had ever encountered and there was a pang of regret in her stomach for making him feel all of those dark days because he was truly spectacular. A one in a million type of man…type of love…God made no mistakes when He'd created him. He was carving out perfection, when He'd made Ethic.

"Very," he added.

"My professor wants to represent me. He has friends in the publishing industry. He gave it to a friend to read and they want to publish it," she said. "He emailed me a week ago about it and I haven't answered."

"You should," Ethic whispered, as he carried her back to shore.

"It's our story, though. It's mine and yours. Those characters are me and you. It feels too personal to share," she admitted. "It feels like people will judge."

"Fuck people," he stated. "Do what you feel."

She didn't unwrap her legs, when they emerged from the water and Ethic took wide steps toward the house. "You gon' make a nigga carry you the whole way?"

She hung on tight and nodded. "Yup. That's the only way I'll make it."

He smiled, a stubborn, half smile and kissed her neck, as he carried her back toward the house. He would carry her, he would shoulder the weight, every burden, all insecurities. Always.

"You gon' call me? Even though you hit twice on the first date?" she asked, amusement dancing in her eyes.

"As good as that shit is, I'm pulling up on you, fuck a phone call."

Alani hollered in laughter and buried her face into his chest, embarrassed, as he carried her into the house. His heart was full, and he hated to admit it, but she was right about the dating thing. It was good for them. It was a piece of their relationship that he hadn't realized was missing. He would be patient with her and jump through all these remedial hoops, one at a time, as long as she needed him to.

CHAPTER 19

Baby, you don't know
What you do to me
Between me and you
I feel a chemistry

Morgan stood in front of the mirror in the rec center and her body was going through the movements, but her mind was a million miles away. Aaliyah oozed through the speakers and Mo felt tears burning her eyes. Aria danced beside her, but Mo wasn't feeling it. She couldn't feel anything but hurt and she froze mid-routine, turning away from the mirror, as she doubled over in grief.

Aria stopped the song and panted, out of breath, as she looked at Mo in sympathy.

"Aww, Mo," she whispered.

"I can't do this, Aria, I can't…" Mo gasped.

Morgan sat right where she stood, in the middle of the wooden dance floor. She pulled her knees to her chest and buried her head on top of them, weeping.

Aria sat beside her, rubbing small circles against her back.

"Mo, what can I do?" she asked.

"I need Ethic," she whispered. "Call him, please."

Morgan was falling apart. She had done that a lot over the years and every time he had put her back together. He knew how to do it, effortlessly. He had memorized where her pieces fit, and she needed him to come put them back in place again because Messiah had destroyed her puzzle.

"Ethic, I need Ethic." She cried it from her soul, panicking, unable to breathe, unable to even see, as the tears blurred her vision. Anxiety attacks. Depression. The dark thoughts that had scared her as a child. It hadn't plagued her in so long that she had thought it to be just a phase that she worked through after losing her sister, but Messiah's lies...Messiah's deceit, was bringing it all back.

"Okay, okay," Aria said, rushing to Morgan's bag and returning with her phone. Morgan grabbed it and unlocked the screen, but her finger lingered over Ethic's name, as a beat of hesitation ceased her.

For so long, they had lived in a state of pain with one another over Raven's death. They were the only two that felt it at such powerful magnitude. He understood. Her pain was his. They had shared the devastation for years and Morgan loved him for feeling it so deeply with her. She loved Ethic with her soul. He was her sister's love...from the first time Morgan had set sights on Ethic, she had loved him. She wanted a man just like him because she had watched him love over the years and no one loved a woman better than Ethic. Messiah was supposed to be that for her. He was supposed to be like her father. He was taught by the very man who had shown her what love looked like. How had he failed so miserably? Morgan wanted to call him so bad, both of them,

Ethic and Messiah, but she didn't. Ethic no longer lived in the shadows. He was no longer grieving in the dark. Alani had pulled him to the light. Ethic was off somewhere loving and living. He was moving on and Morgan thought she was too, but Morgan would forever be cloaked in despair. The one shot she had taken at reviving her heart had backfired. She ended up in the bed of her enemy, in the crosshairs of Mizan's brother. Morgan just wanted it all to go away. It was eating away at her.

"Mo? Do you want me to call him for you?" Aria asked, kneeling and looking at Morgan in concern.

Morgan stood abruptly to her feet. "No, I just need to get out of here. Fuck this. Fuck all this shit," she said, rushing to grab her bag.

"Mo!" Aria shouted.

Morgan turned, just as she got to the door. She shook her head, as tears streamed down her face.

"You make sure Messiah knows that everything is all fucked up because of him…that this is all his fault."

CHAPTER 20

You're so patient with me," Alani whispered, as he pulled up to the curb in front of her house. The entire four-hour ride had been silent. Alani was satisfied in ways she didn't know a woman could be satisfied. She was also moody. She was filled with guilt to the max. She had to will her eyes not to shed tears the entire way, while gripping Ethic's hand, desperately, on the way back to Flint. Thoughts of her daughter ran rampant in her mind, while Ethic ran wild and free in her heart. Her soul was at war. It was a tug of war over what she deserved. She couldn't love on a ghost, however; she couldn't wrap her arms around a memory. Ethic was her biggest sin and she was committed to sinning daily, even through moments like this one when it hurt. "Some days, I give you all of me. Others, I'm terrified to give you even a piece, and you stay through it all. You keep coming back to love me on days when I don't even love me. You notice, and you compensate for everything I'm drained of." She looked at him in amazement. Ethic wiped a hand down the back of his neck and glanced out the window.

"I'll take whatever you giving me. Anger, love, resentment. I'll eat that, as long as you're here. I've felt what it's like to not have you. That can't happen again," he said, without looking at her.

"What if we're forcing something that was never supposed to be?" she asked. Those words jarred his attention.

Alani looked down, as she fumbled with her fingers. She was inside her head, contemplating one of the biggest moves she had ever made with a man in her life. She wanted him. She wanted him all the time and the pit in her stomach, from pulling up to her house, was proof enough that he wasn't supposed to be dropping her off at all. He captured her nervous fingers in his palm, bringing her hand to his lips.

"Is it crazy that it hurts to pull up to my own house? Just thinking about packing up Eazy and Bella and handing them off to you and watching y'all drive away without me makes me feel sick," she whispered.

Ethic reached one hand across the car to grip the back of her headrest, as he turned his body toward her.

"I thought this was what you wanted? Dating. A little distance. Pace things out so we can get to know one another," Ethic answered, perplexed. He could feel the tension building in the center of his forehead. Women. They said one thing but meant another.

"I know you, Ethic," she whispered.

She shook her head, confused. She was being bombarded by so many different emotions.

"Taking shit slow don't mean we're stopping," he said. Ethic wanted to throw caution to the wind and go with his original plan. Straight to the next stop. Marriage and babies. Change her last name and her zip code, but Alani was fickle.

She was emotional and damaged. Her needs changed daily. Her intentions changed hourly. He wanted her to be sure. He needed to be sure. The decisions they made affected his children, at this point, and he couldn't put them through anymore inconsistency. "I wasn't with it at first, but let's just see it through. Let's allow Nyair to get us through it, because as much as you try to hide it, I can still see the hate inside you."

Alani sucked in air and held it to try to fill the empty pit in her. "I don't hate you." She shook her head in disappointment, in shame. She had handled so many things with him poorly. "You don't deserve that. I don't hate you. I hate that you even think that. You can't love someone that you think feels that way about you."

He pinched her chin and drew her near, kissing her lips. One quick peck, his full lips meeting hers, then pulling back slightly to lick his lips, before kissing her again. His tongue in her mouth reminded her of his tongue in other places and Alani melted.

"It don't matter. Hate, love, I want every part," he said. "Things play out the way they do for a reason, but me and you, we're going to be fine."

"What if-"

He pulled her to him, again, silencing her with kisses that made her soul stir. "I'm going to make sure we make it this time. That part ain't your job. It's mine and I'ma do a damned good job, baby. Trust me," Ethic assured.

She nodded. Putting her faith in a man like Ethic was effortless. He did exactly what he said he would. There was no anticipation of let down with him, no fear that he wouldn't come through. He opened his door and climbed out the car and then walked around the front of the car to get to the passenger side. He opened the door and she stepped out.

She led the way up to her home, the home he had paid to remodel. She glanced up the block at all the homes that had been restored because of him, because he had cared enough to make a change to her small community…because he thought her worthy enough to live in a safe, clean, environment. Ethic reached the door and turned back to find her standing there, halfway up her walkway, staring at him like he was a beautiful sunset. In awe.

"You coming?" he asked.

This nigga here. He had no idea what he did to her. The natural charisma of him just attracted her. He wasn't cocky or entitled. It was like Ethic didn't even realize how handsome he was. He didn't know that the seat of women's panties moistened whenever he entered a room.

She nodded and then joined him, removing her keys from her handbag. She held it up for him and he grabbed it and then opened the door.

He held open the door, and as she passed him she said, "Keep it. I want you to have access to everything. I want to live with you, but until I can, until we're ready, I want you to be able to come and go whenever you want." She gave him a peck on his parted lips and wrapped both hands around his neck, as she looked up at him. "If you want to stop by for breakfast, you're welcome. Don't call, just come." She rubbed the back of his neck and then kissed him deeper, pulling his bottom lip into her mouth this time. "If you wake up in the middle of the night and your dick is hard, you come through." He groaned, as he gripped her ass with one hand. She slipped her tongue into his mouth, feeling him harden against her body. He pulled her into him and she moaned. "If you want to come eat my pussy until I scream, you pull up on me. Anytime," she whispered.

"How about now? I'm trying to put my face in it now," he groaned. The sounds of Bella and Eazy traveled from upstairs and she smiled.

"Not now. I miss it, but I miss them more," she giggled. She turned and then headed for the living room, leaving him standing there, adjusting his dick so that his kids wouldn't see what she had done to him.

"Hello?" she called out. "We're back!"

The sound of feet racing down the wooden staircase filled the air.

"Yay! They're back!" Eazy shouted. He ran right into Alani, wrapping her in a tight hug. Alani laughed and hugged him right back.

"Get off my woman, homie. I'm starting to think I've got some competition," Ethic said, noticing how smitten his son was with Alani.

Alani winked at him, as Bella came waltzing into the room with her iPhone in hand, ears plugged with headphones.

"Hey, Daddy. Hey, Alani," she greeted.

"Where's Nannie?" Alani asked.

"On the back patio, playing cards with Mr. Larry," Bella said.

Ethic lifted a brow. "Her boyfriend, but if she ever hears you say it, it'll be the last thing you ever utter," Alani snickered.

Ethic nodded. "Y'all ready?" he asked.

"Can I stay?" Bella asked. "Or Alani, can you come with us?"

"B…she's busy. We've taken up enough of her time," Ethic interrupted.

Out of nowhere, Nannie's voice boomed. "She ain't got nothing to do but play hard to get. Quit making that man chase you and get your narrow behind out of here. I'm fine here by myself. I've been getting around just fine without you for 75 years. I don't need no babysitter," Nannie fussed. Mr. Larry followed behind her, coming into view. Nannie walked up to Ethic and kissed his cheek. "Hey, handsome," she greeted. "Lord knows He broke the mold when He made you."

Ethic blushed, and Alani cocked her neck back, but she didn't dare utter one word. "Ethic, this is Mr. Larry. He's a friend from the church. Larry, this is Ethic, Alani's boyfriend."

Alani knew how Ethic felt about the term. It was childish, and it put expectations on them.

"Nannie! He's not my-"

"Alani, come off it already," Nannie fussed. "What? He done got you a ring? Because unless he's your fiancé now? He's definitely your boyfriend. Damn man been your boyfriend since you gave him that pie, and I ain't talking about the one I baked either," she said, giving Alani the side eye.

"What pie?" Eazy asked. "I want pie."

Ethic snickered and extended his hand. The older man shook it.

"Nice to meet you, sir," Ethic greeted. "I'm the boyfriend, although I wouldn't mind the upgrade. I like how you think, Ms. Pat."

Alani blushed.

"What pie?" Eazy asked, again.

"Boy, come on," Bella said, as she pushed him forward toward the door. "They not talking about pie, pie…they talking about-"

"Umm, little girl," Alani interrupted. "You better think we talking about pie, pie too!"

Ethic turned his head toward his daughter. "What she said," he added, frowning. Bella had been losing her mind lately. He hadn't missed the slick comments she had been making and it bothered him. She was growing up; sex, and boys, and makeup, were infiltrating her world. Ethic felt the tension build in him and he rubbed the back of his neck. Bella tucked her lips inside her mouth, knowing when to stop while she was ahead, and walked out the front door.

Nannie laughed, as she saw the entire bunch to the door.

"Call me if you need anything," Alani said. "I'll be home tomorrow, I guess."

"Mmm hmm… bye, child," Nannie said, ushering her out the door.

"Relax," Ethic whispered, as he kissed the side of her head. "I'll hire a nurse first thing in the morning. Someone good that you're comfortable with."

"A nurse? Ethic, it's only for a night," Alani protested.

"Let me take you home, baby," he said. Just from the way he said it, she knew he was talking about forever. Fuck dating. Moments ago, they had decided to take it slow, now he was putting his foot on the gas pedal, speeding in the fast lane. Neither Ethic or Alani knew the path to their destination. They didn't even know the speed limit to get there, all they knew was that they should end up together...the destination was love...they were guessing their way there, hoping they would get there in one piece.

Alani looked up at him and then out at Bella and Eazy, as they made their way into the backseat of Ethic's car.

"Home?" she asked. Her heart fluttered, unsurely. It was such a huge step. Such a commitment. Was he saying what she thought he was saying? Pushing her into the next level of their relationship. *What if we don't make it? But what if we do? He could see the thoughts overwhelming her.*

"With me, with us," he said, as he motioned for the truck. "Make a home with me, Alani. It's just bricks and plaster without you. Make a man out of me," he said. Alani felt like she couldn't breathe. You just didn't go from a first date to living together. You just didn't.

He kissed her lips and she withered under his touch. Her entire spirit glowed with him, when she allowed it to, when she let go of the hurt, he was the very best medicine for her ailments. "Can we do this?" she asked.

Out of nowhere, Nannie stuck her head out the open living room window, the one Mr. Larry was there to fix.

"Yes, damn it. Yes, your difficult-ass can do this. Give the man a break! I swear you want to be lonely!"

Alani's chin hit her chest, as Ethic chuckled.

"Take her ass home, Ezra. Gone now," Nannie urged.

"I respect my elders," he told Alani, with amusement playing at his lips. She shook her head, smiling, but feeling flutters inside, and she wondered if it was her intuition telling her to decline, warning her that this was too big of a step. Nannie had never been one to bite her tongue. She gave no never mind about Alani's embarrassment. "I do what I'm told." He took her hand, as they headed home, to their home, together. They were finally giving it a real shot as a couple, under one roof. Alani was both excited and terrified.

CHAPTER 21

organ sat inside one of Ethic's old-school, refurbished cars with her head resting against the leather seat. Earbuds plugged her ears, and the music drowned out the hum of the engine.

I had high hopes for us, baby
Like I was on dope for us, baby
Chasin' after a high that I'llllll never get back again
So we turn into threeee long years
And it became painfully clear that weeee
We would never see those dayss againnnn
But I guess forrrever, doesn't last too long foreverrrr
Doesn't last too long forever
Doesn't last too long these days

She closed her eyes and placed both hands over her heart, as she felt the steady thump as it beat. Her face was wet. Messiah had hurt her. It was an overwhelming and unending feeling. She had felt it before when her father had died, then again, when her mother had died, then Raven. Why did this feel like death? Messiah's betrayal felt like the end of the world, so why not end it? The exhaust tube that rested in the driver's side window was connected to the tailpipe of the car. She could smell the fumes from the exhaust, as it backed up inside the cabin of the car. She was breathing it in. She had done the research. It was the least painful way to go. It would end it all. It would take away the ache and she wouldn't feel a thing. She would just fall asleep, and when her family found her, it would look like she was resting. Eazy and Bella wouldn't be afraid if they found her first. Ethic and Alani would come home from their trip to discover what she had done. It wouldn't be gruesome. She would no longer be in anyone's way. It was perfect. Morgan's lips stretched in grief, as she sobbed. How someone could pretend to love her so perfectly was beyond her. If his fake love had felt that good, what would his real love feel like? Why couldn't she have him? Why did he have to lie? How could he want to hurt her? She would have never hurt him. Even now after discovering his deception, she didn't wish harm on him. She just couldn't go back to living without him. She didn't want to. Life wasn't the same if he wasn't in it. Morgan grabbed her phone from the passenger seat and went to Messiah's contact information. Her finger lingered over his name. If she could just hear his voice. If he would just answer her calls, she could get out of this car. Just a connection...just a hello would make her feel like she mattered to him, but every time she called she was sent to voicemail.

He doesn't care anymore.

She dialed his number, and this time, she wasn't even given the courtesy of a ring. The automated voice came on immediately, as if she had been blocked. Morgan's lip trembled, and she placed both hands on the steering wheel, as tears trailed down her face. She sucked in a deep breath. Inhaling poison, trying to speed up this process. At that very moment, Morgan just wanted her daddy. She wanted to close her eyes and wake up wherever Benjamin Atkins was...wherever they all were...her family...that's where she wanted to be. Death felt like going home. A reunion that she had avoided for years. Instead of embracing it, she had run from death. She had been afraid of it, feeling like the inevitable would eventually catch up to her. Now, she was chasing it. She wished for it because life had gotten heavy. Morgan wasn't like other people. She couldn't withstand this pain. She wasn't strong... not without him. He was her muscle and he was gone. Morgan picked up her phone and went to Twitter. She scheduled a tweet. Every Friday at 1:00 a.m. she wanted to let the world know.

M&M Forever.

She felt her heart slow and she clicked out of her phone and then leaned her head back against the seat. Her neck was weak, like her head weighed 1000 pounds. She sighed, as her eye lids fluttered. Damn. They were heavy too. *If I could just hear his voice. If he would just answer.* Morgan went to reach for her phone, one last time, but her arm was now heavy too and her heart, damn, that was heavy too. It took so much effort for her breaths to lift her chest.

"Hey, Stank."

Morgan saw Raven signing to her in her mind.

"You've got to wake up, Mo. Don't you dare give up. Fight, Morgan."

Morgan felt agony, suddenly, as she was overwhelmed with the urge to push the pipe from the window, but she couldn't move.

I can't, Rae. I can't fight.

"Get up! Morgan, wake up!"

This time, it wasn't Raven's voice she heard. It was Ethic's and he was screaming it desperately, roaring at her with such fear in his tone that Morgan wanted to listen. It was too late, however. She couldn't. She just couldn't. She had no strength. Her eyes were mere slits, as she tried to force them to open wide, but she only saw Ethic through a sliver and then he disappeared as the blackness behind her lids took her under. She was gone.

CHAPTER 22

Mo?" Bella called, as she saw Ethic emerge from the garage, carrying Morgan in his arms. "What's wrong with her?" Bella asked. "Mo!"

"Oh my god," Alani whispered, as she hopped from the passenger side. "Ethic! What happened? What happened?!"

"Call 911!" he shouted, as he laid Morgan out on the ground.

Alani's fingers trembled, as she dialed for help. She handed the phone to Bella. "You tell them the address and tell them your sister is here, unconscious, and we need an ambulance." Bella's eyes watered, as she tried to get out of the car. Alani pushed against the back door. "Bella, no!" she said, sternly. Bella's eyes were gazing pass Alani, up the driveway to Morgan's body on the ground. Alani snapped her fingers in front of her face, jarring Bella's attention. "Bella. This is important. Get help here now and don't get out of this car. Keep Eazy inside."

"Is she going to be okay?" Bella asked, eyes full of tears.

Eazy stood, gripping the headrest of the driver's seat to try to peek through the windshield. "What's wrong with Mo?"

Alani nodded. "I'm going to help her, but I need you to help too, by staying here with Eazy, okay?"

Tears rolled down Bella's face, as a familiar feeling crept into her soul. Flashes of Raven lived in her…that day…so long ago…when she had been killed. Bella had been young but it was a day she would never forget. She remembered Ethic crying over Raven much like he was crying over Morgan now. Raven had died that day, and terror seized her, as she wondered if Mo was dying too.

"Bella. Take the phone, baby girl. We need help." Bella took the phone. Alani reached across the seat and hastily opened Eazy's backpack.

"Eazy, baby, play with your iPad, okay?" She closed them safely inside, behind the dark tint of the truck and then ran to Ethic and Morgan.

"Mo, wake up, baby girl! Wake up for me!" he pleaded, as he hovered over her, hands on top of each other, as he jerked downward, giving her chest compressions.

"What happened?" Alani shrieked, as she came to her knees. Alani's eyes scoured Morgan. She was looking for blood, clues, any indication of what had occurred. "Ethic!" Alani looked to the open garage and her eyes widened in horror when she saw the make shift gas chamber. "Oh my god. Ethic, she needs oxygen. How long was she in there?"

"I don't know!" he shouted.

One. Two. Three. Four. Five…Ethic counted to 30 in his head, pumping her heart, as he gritted his teeth in desperation.

He pinched her nose and blew air into her mouth.

"I'll do the compressions, Ethic. You're pressing too hard. You'll break her ribs," Alani said, but Ethic didn't stop. He was distraught, as he tried to make Morgan's heart beat again. Pressing harder and harder with every pump of his strong arms.

One. Two. Three. Four. Five...30 compressions...hard, forceful blows to Mo's chest because he was filled with angst and needed this to work...he needed her heart to beat... needed her to breathe.

"Ethic, you're going to hurt her," Alani pleaded. When Ethic moved to Morgan's mouth to give her air, Alani mounted Morgan's body, placing her hands over Morgan's chest.

"One, two, three, four, five..." All the way to 30. "Breathe for her, Ethic," she said, urgently, but in control. She had done this before. At the hospice she used to work at. It was second nature for her. "Every 30 seconds you give her air. Two breaths."

Alani closed her eyes and prayed, as she did the next set of compressions. *God, please cover her. Please...please... please...No more losses. God, please! She doesn't deserve this.* Alani's eyes burned with conviction.

The sirens in the distance did little to ease the tension in Alani's chest.

"Come on, Mo, come on," Ethic whispered, as he leaned over her, absolutely destroyed. "You can do it, baby girl, just wake up."

"One, two, three, four, five..." All the way to 30. "Breathe," Alani whispered, frantically.

"It's not working. She's not waking up," Ethic said, through gritted teeth. "Baby girl don't do this to me! Get up, Mo!" Ethic's voice was angry, tortured and the sight of him made Alani even more distraught. Alani had never thought it was possible for a person to love a child that wasn't biologically theirs the same way you loved your own, but seeing him like this...Alani knew that Morgan was his child through and through.

"We just have to keep her heart pumping until help gets here," Alani said, more to herself then to Ethic. Her fear-filled voice cracked. Morgan was so unresponsive, and Alani felt no life energy coming from her. She prayed Morgan wasn't already gone. The ambulance's alarm wailed, as it pulled onto Ethic's estate, and as they approached, Ethic said, "Keep her heart beating for me, Lenika. You have God in you, baby. She needs you." The way he looked at her. The hopelessness. The fear. He was pleading...begging her to help this girl he loved so much. He was depending on her. *I'm not a doctor,* she thought, fear-stricken, not wanting to be responsible if his oldest child died in her hands.

"Ma'am, we've got it from here," the paramedics said. Alani kept compressing.

"One. Two. Three. Four. Five..." all the way to 30. Her arms burned, she was exhausted, but she couldn't stop...wouldn't stop, because Ethic had asked her not to.

She went to Morgan's mouth. *Breathe.* She blew air into her lungs. The way Morgan's chest rose artificially, only rising because Alani was forcing a spurt of life into her, made Alani's eyes mist. Morgan Atkins, this beautiful girl, a piece of Ethic's heart, was undoubtedly lifeless.

"I've got it. I'm certified, just do the rest," Alani insisted, as she pumped Morgan's heart.

"Ma'am..."

Alani glanced at Ethic who sat on the ground, elbows to knees, hands on the top of his head, in distress, and her heart ached...it bled for him. God, she loved him and he loved Morgan so it meant she loved Morgan too. They couldn't lose her. "I'm not stopping! Just do the rest!"

The paramedics went to work around Alani, hoisting both Alani and Morgan up onto a stretcher, as Alani kept the compressions going. She had been at it so long that her arms had Charlie horses, and she was sweating, but she continued. Ethic stood, rushing alongside the stretcher, watching Alani's dainty hands tensing against Morgan's chest.

He couldn't follow them onto the bed of the ambulance, however. Alani looked up at him, eyes shining in fear, tears on her cheeks, as she kept the count.

One. Two. Three. Four. Five...all the way to 30.

"Daddy!"

Ethic heard Bella, screaming for him from the car, but he couldn't tear his eyes off Mo.

"Ethic, I've got her. Take care of them. Take them back to Nannie and meet me at the hospital. I won't leave her side until you get there," she promised.

He nodded, feeling helpless. He placed both hands on his head, his face wrinkled in agony, eyes clouding...a man destroyed. The paramedics closed the steel doors and the ambulance pulled away with two of his most precious girls trapped inside.

Bella sprang from the backseat of that truck like she was in a race and someone had yelled, "go!" As soon as the ambulance departed, Bella was at Ethic's side.

"Where are they taking her? What happened to her?" Bella cried.

"She's hurt, B. She hurt herself," Ethic whispered, in disbelief. He rushed, ushering her back to the car, but his legs were weakening. He leaned over the hood of his car, hands gripping the edge.

"Fuck!" he shouted, causing Bella to jump and Eazy to climb from the truck. His balled fists slammed against the metal, as the anguish traveled through him.

"Daddy?" Eazy's voice caused Ethic to steel. He could never feel without interruption. He could never just go through the motions of his emotions. They were always concealed, always guarded, always bubbling beneath the surface because he had little eyes watching him, learning from him, depending on him. His son's voice was a reminder and Ethic reserved himself and stood up straight, sniffing away his worry, as he flicked his nose and turned to face his children.

"She's fine, Big Man. Mo's going to be just fine. Climb in the car," Ethic said.

"Where are we going?" Eazy asked.

"Back to Nannie's," Ethic said. "I've got to check on Mo. I'll be back for you in a few hours." He had done it. He had concealed the storm that was moving through his body to protect his children.

Eazy was easy to pacify but Bella stood there, looking up at him defiantly.

"I'm coming with you," Bella said. "We can drop Eazy off, but I'm coming to the hospital. She's my sister…"

Ethic nodded, almost losing it, as his chin quivered, and he pulled Bella into his chest, kissing the top of her head as he cried.

"It's going to be okay, Daddy," Bella whispered, as she buried herself into his chest, wrapping her arms around his waist. "She's strong. You taught us to be strong. It doesn't always have to be you."

Damn it if Bella wasn't acting like the parent in this moment. Her words put the vigor back in his legs and the hope back in his heart. Ethic kissed the top of her head. He blinked back emotion. "Let's go."

Alani stood outside the glass window, looking inside the room, as anxiety ate away at her stomach. The sound of the door opening behind her caused her to turn and when she saw him, she ran to him, wrapping her arms around him, instantly. She quickly pulled back and bent down to hug Bella.

"Where is she?" Ethic asked, urgently.

"She's alive, Ethic. She's breathing. They're giving her hyperbaric oxygen therapy to remove the carbon monoxide from her body. No one knows how long she was there, though, Ethic. There could be…" she paused, as she looked down at Bella, not wanting to divulge too much. She lowered sympathetic eyes to the floor and took his hands. She leaned into his ear and finished. "Brain damage," she whispered. Ethic collapsed into her, sobbing. Alani held him, her soft hands rubbing his head and face, as she kissed his lips, feeling so broken because he was so broken. His children had been through so much. He had been through so much. It was just one thing after another.

"Shh," she soothed. "Baby…"

"Should we pray?"

Both Alani and Ethic turned to Bella, in surprise. "If it's that bad, we should pray, right?"

"Little girl," Alani whispered, in amazement, as she opened up their circle, motioning for Bella to join the embrace. "The soul God gave you is miraculous." Alani, Ethic, and Bella stood in a circle, arms wrapped around one another. Alani fixed her mouth to begin but Bella was already speaking.

"God, it's me, Bella, but You probably already know that. I'm a little nervous or scared…or both." Alani gave Bella's hand a squeeze. "My sister needs You. My whole family needs You. I know You save people because I prayed for You to save Alani and You did." Alani looked up at Bella, with fresh pools of emotion in her eyes. Bella's eyes were squeezed tight, but Alani felt Ethic's gaze on her, she turned to meet his stare. "I prayed for You to save my daddy and he's still here too. Then, I prayed that they would love one another, and now they do. I just have one more favor, God. Please, heal Mo. Please don't let her die. Whatever the doctors are saying might be wrong with her, take it away. Protect our family. We have a lot of hard days. Can You make some of them easier? Please. We need each other, and we just got Alani. You can't take Mo. We just want to be complete. I need everyone to be safe. Amen."

"Amen, baby girl," Alani said. She let go of Ethic's hand and focused all her attention on Bella, as she hugged her. "That was a beautiful prayer. You're a beautiful girl and we're going to be okay. I know it took me a while to come around, but I'm not leaving you, or your daddy, or Eazy, or Morgan. Nothing will make me leave ever again. Morgan is going to be fine. God will make us whole, just trust Him."

Ethic stood at the window, looking into the room where Morgan was being held inside the pressurized chamber. He gripped the edge and stood with his head bowed, his strong back, tense, as the weight of the world sat on his shoulders. Alani could see it, the pressure, of holding his entire family together...alone. It had been his responsibility for so long. A man raising three children. He had just lost his fourth and now his oldest was in jeopardy. Alani grabbed Bella's hand and led her over to Ethic. She placed a hand on his back, as she stepped beside him. Standing between two Okafors, she knew they needed her just as much as she needed them. If Morgan Atkins died, nothing would ever be the same... for any of them...another moth... another flame...The thought alone paralyzed Ethic. He needed God. He prayed desperately for a miracle, because if Morgan never opened her eyes again, Ethic would close his too…a father wasn't supposed to bury his children. His heart wouldn't be able to endure the loss of another Atkins girl…*God, please, not again…*

TO BE CONTINUED...
IN THE FINAL BOOK...
ETHIC V